Praise for

Sandwich, with a Side of Romance

"In *Sandwich, With a Side of Romance*, Krista Phillips will win you over with her witty, entertaining, laugh-out-loud writing style. She's created loveable, quirky, down-to-earth characters with real life struggles. As the characters wrestle to overcome their problems, you'll find yourself cheering them on and savoring the sweet but sassy romance that ends with a blissful sigh."

— Jody Hedlund, best-selling author of *The Preacher's Bride*

"With lovable characters, an engaging plot, and a swoon-worthy romance, debut author Krista Phillips has penned a novel that will have readers laughing and flipping pages well into the night. *Sandwich, With a Side of Romance* is a refreshing and enjoyable read!"

— Katie Ganshert, award-winning author of
A Broken Kind of Beautiful

"Don't let the light-hearted cover and title fool you. Krista Phillips' spunky, rough-around-the-edges heroine may be "tickle me" funny, but her faith journey offers more than a cute read. There is depth here, made all the more satisfying served up with a generous side of romance."

— Tamara Leigh, bestselling author of *Lady Of Eve*
and the Age of Faith series

A (kinda) Country Christmas

Other books by Krista Phillips:

Sandwich, With a Side of Romance
A Side of Faith
A Side of Hope
A Side of Love

The Engagement Plot

A (kinda) Country Christmas
A (sorta) Southern Serenade
A (nearly) Normal Nanny
A (wildly) Wonderful Wedding

Match Me If You Can

A (kinda) Country Christmas

Krista Phillips

ONE WOMAN'S DREAM
PUBLISHING

A (kinda) Country Christmas

Copyright © 2015 by Krista Phillips

ISBN: 0692552219
ISBN-13: 978-0692552216

Published by -

One Woman's Dream
www.kristaphillips.com

Printed in the United States of America

Dedication

To Robert and Linda – my fabulous father-and-mother-in-law.

You welcomed this strange Hoosier into your family sixteen years ago and showed me lots of love and grace.

You embraced me, regardless of our differences in accent and traditions, and I will always be forever thankful for you both! You've been such a blessing to me and my whole family!

Love you bunches!

Krista Phillips

1

"T'is the season to be Jolly!" Sadie Jenkins belted out the Christmas tune, not caring that the notes were a little off-key or that her teenage daughter was on the opposite side of the store, covering her ears and grimacing. In fact, just to add a dash of fun, she upped the decibel a bit as she continued. "Fa-la-la-la-la-la-la-la-la. Don we now our—"

"I'm gonna don my coat and leave if you don't stop, Mom."

Sadie laughed while she hung what seemed like the thousandth—and definitely last—ornament on the ten foot tree that stood in the center of Bethlehem's Boutique, the family-owned Christmas store just off the parkway in Gatlinburg, Tennessee. "Stop being such a party pooper, Maribelle. I'm just trying to spread a little Christmas cheer. Besides, the shop opens in about thirty minutes anyway, so your ears will be safe then."

"And what does that say about your parenting skills that you care more about your customers than your own daughter?"

She took a deep breath and exhaled, begging God for

patience in dealing with her daughter. When Mari was born, Sadie had thought if she could just get past the crying-all-night stage, the rest of it would be a breeze.

Then during the terrible twos-threes-and-fours, she swore that if only they could get past the temper tantrums, all would be well in the world of parenting.

But that morphed into the high-pitched screeches and wails that only a little girl could perfect, followed closely on its heels by puberty and raging hormonal changes that almost drove a momma to drink something harder than sweet tea.

She'd been warned of all those stages though.

What no one had ever mentioned was the torture that was her only daughter at eighteen.

Gone were the childish screams of "That's not fair" or "I hate you" or "You don't love me" and in their place was a pompous young lady who was way too smart for her own good, who criticized her mother's every move, who made her mission in life to do every single thing her mother did *not* want her to do out of pure spite.

Sadie should have been prepared. Truth be told, she had it coming, considering she was only thirty-four and had conceived sweet Maribelle during one of those teenage rebellious moments herself.

Biting back a reply that would only make things worse, she stepped back to survey the tree. "What do you think, Mari? Is it too much?"

Maribelle maneuvered around the various Christmas displays to stand beside her mother. She shrugged. "It's fine."

"Just fine?" The center tree was the focal point of the shop and Sadie's pride and joy. Fine was not an option.

Her daughter shrugged. "I like a little color. I told you that two months ago when you asked my opinion on the concept. Remember? When you ignored me and did what you wanted anyway like always?"

Sadie frowned. If anyone was guilty of doing whatever

they wanted these days, it was Mari.

Taking a step back, she eyed the tree with a critical eye. It was a little plain, but in a modern, sophisticated way. The fake evergreen, its green needles lightly frosted, twinkled with the silver, white and clear glass ornaments, with doves and white sprigs of flowers tying the look together. The silver glass star at the top was like the shimmering icing on the cake.

She was going for elegant, southern chic, but Mari had told her in no uncertain terms that the idea was dumb. Red plus green equaled Christmas.

But the rest of the store screamed red and green and country Christmas, so shouldn't the centerpiece of the displays stand out as different and eye catching? "Well, I like it."

"And as we all know, that's all that counts." Mari mumbled the flippant reply as she grabbed her ear buds from the counter and headed into the backroom.

Sadie rested her hands on her hips and took deep breaths.

In.

Out.

It was the Saturday morning after Thanksgiving. The day she earmarked to begin celebrating Christmas. The season tended to get muddled with the rest of the year since her store did Christmas year-round in one of the Smoky Mountain's most famous tourist towns. Nothing was going to rain on her parade today. She would sing hokey Christmas carols at the top of her lungs, regardless of accuracy, until the shop opened, then zip it and let her iPod entertain the customers.

Mari was just in a funk today. She'd get over it. Just like all the other seasons had passed by with neither of them worse for wear, this one would too.

Except—next year, Mari would be off to college. She should have gone this year, but Sadie had convinced her waiting a year to go to college would be wise. She could save up money and not go as deeply in debt.

So come next year, Sadie would be left—here. Alone.

Flicking away the depressing thought, she started in on an even louder opera version of "We Wish You a Merry Christmas," hoping the words would drown out all the anxiety that was so present these days.

She sang and flitted through the room, fixing wayward decorations, adjusting wreaths, and making sure all lights were shining brightly.

She'd just started a second go around of, "Oh Christmas Tree" when she heard a tapping on the window.

Whipping around to the storefront, she almost dropped the angel ornament in her hand.

Peering into the store was a man.

A drop-dead gorgeous man dressed in a fancy looking black coat and a stocking cap pulled over his head. A short, trimmed beard completed the look.

He was *hot* as Mari would say. Well, Sadie too, but she tried to frown on the use of the word, because that's what good mothers do, right? It's what hers had done.

But in her head, she applied the word liberally, especially to the man who was squinting through the frosted door decoration and turning to leave.

Her pulse galloped at Polar Express speed. Leave? Running to the door, she turned back the deadbolt. She tried to calm her voice as she called to the figure retreating down the sidewalk. "Sorry, we're just now—opening." That sounded normal, right? No heavy breathing from having just run across a store full of very expensive breakables....

The man turned and smiled, revealing a wide jaw and the cutest dimple she'd ever seen. "No problem. I was just out for a walk this morning to kill some time. I can come back later."

"Nonsense. I was just fixin' to flip the sign to open." To prove her point, she reached beside the door and turned the two-sided chalkboard sign around so the curly

A (kinda) Country Christmas

Open faced the street. "See?"

His mouth curved into a smile. "Well, thank you—" he paused and glanced down to her apron where her name was embroidered, then quickly back to her eyes. "—Sadie. I think I'll come and take a look then."

Sugarplums danced in her stomach as she stepped aside to allow him in. When he passed and his back was to her, she pressed a hand to the red apron and tugged, making sure it was smooth, then ran her fingers through her blond hair, praying her bangs were behaving today.

"Nice shop you have here."

She turned and smiled when she saw him in front of the center tree, holding one of the clear, glass bulbs. "Thank you. Our family is a bit fanatical about Christmas you'd say, so it's in my blood. My parents opened the store almost nineteen years ago now, but I run it now along with my daughter." Why was she blabbering on about such nonsense? He didn't care two licks about the ownership of the hand-me-down store.

He replaced the ornament. "You're a native to the area, then?"

"Oh goodness no. My family moved here when I was sixteen." No need to mention that her parents were moving her away from her deadbeat, drug-addicted eighteen-year-old boyfriend after they found out she was pregnant with his baby. "We're actually from Southern Indiana originally. My uncle willed this lot to my dad years ago, so given their insane love of Christmas, they thought it'd be fun to start a little touristy shop here. And the rest, as they say, is history." And needed to stay that way.

"That would explain your accent, then. A little southern—but not quite."

"I still *reckon* and *declare* every once in a while. What about you? Do I detect a little New York there?" It was hard to pinpoint. Really, the man hardly had an accent at all.

"Probably. I grew up there, but I do a lot of traveling

for business, so you never know what crazy accent I might pick up on. I actually spent the last few months in Beijing."

"Wow. That's—that must have been an interesting experience." A world traveler. So different than her own humble existence that was comprised of living in two touristy cities her whole life, with occasional trips to the Atlantic coast for vacations. Whoopty-do.

"It's pretty cool, I admit. But it can get old after a while, too."

He had no idea what *old after a while* meant. Talk to her after he'd been surrounded by Christmas for thirty-four years. Not that she didn't love Christmas. She did. It just— yeah. She was tempted to open a fireworks store someday, just to throw in a little variety. "So where do you call home?"

"I don't. My company's headquarters is in New York, but I'm rarely there, so just do a temporary rent when I'm in town. I do have a vacation house on the coast in South Carolina, so I guess that's home."

Vacation house? Coast? *Swoon.*

Okay. She needed to stop. She was a grown woman, trying to parent a teenager, and most certainly not in the market for a guy who was a nomad. There couldn't be a more opposite man for her. Mari needed her, and she'd promised herself years ago that she'd focus all of her time and energy on her little girl and not be taken in by a *bad boy* again.

Besides, a man's bank account balance shouldn't mean a thing to her. Regardless of the fact that she had no clue how she was going to pay for Mari's college next year. They'd figure it out. They always did.

As if on cue, Mari appeared at Sadie's side. "You opened the store already, Mom? We don't open for another—"

Planting an elbow in her daughter's side, she smiled. "Did you finish in the backroom dear?"

"Finish what? I was just—"

The girl could not take a hint. "The back shelf of ornaments needs straightening up next, then."

Mari glanced at the customer, who was examining the tree, obviously pretending not to listen, then back to Sadie. "Oh. I get it. Flirting again, Mom? Nice."

Sadie's mouth dropped.

The customer coughed.

And Mari smiled, twirled around, her long, blond hair flicking Sadie in the face, and headed to the back of the store.

Nate Meyers replaced the glass angel he'd been pretending to be interested in back onto the tree and turned to watch the younger version of Sadie stalk away, her wavy blond hair bouncing behind her.

He hadn't really gotten a flirting vibe off the girl's mom, and he was usually a pretty good judge of that. But at least she'd helped clarify his curiosity about her mother's marital status.

He definitely wasn't in the market though, despite his meddling sister who insisted he should be.

No woman would want to be tied to a guy who wasn't even in one place long enough to have a home.

No sane woman anyway.

Glancing back at the shopkeeper, he instantly felt pity. Her cheeks were painted with a red blush as she stared after her daughter, her mouth parted in shock. "That's your daughter, I presume?"

Her head jerked back to him as if she'd just remembered his existence. "Um, yes. I—"

"I would have guessed you were sisters. You don't look old enough to be her mom."

She glanced around and started to rearrange a porcelain nativity scene that had been fine how it was. "I was pretty young when I had her."

Reaching out, he squeezed her shoulder. "Listen. Don't worry about what she said."

Glancing at his hand, she frowned and looked up at him. "Excuse me?"

Snatching his hand back, he wished he could kick himself. The old Nate was at it again. The womanizer who used smooth words and expertly placed touches to woo a woman—most times ending up in his bed.

Even though that was the farthest thing from his mind right now, old habits died hard.

He hadn't been that guy for over five years.

There had just been something about the hurt in Sadie's face that made him want to fix it, but she was definitely not the type of woman who was okay with even innocent contact with a strange man.

"I'm sorry. I just meant, don't worry about it. I'm used to that kind of thing."

She turned full to him, fists propped to her trim but nicely curved hips, her blue eyes blazing with fury. "For your information, I was *not* flirting with you."

"I never said—" His words replayed in his mind. Man. He'd sounded like an egotistical jerk. "I'm sorry. I just meant—"

"Oh, I think I know what you meant." She stepped toward him, a shepherd clutched in her hand. He instinctively stepped back. "You poor, rich man have women falling all over you day in and day out and so of course I don't need to worry about falling for your sexy physique and wildly handsome face because you are used to females not being able to control themselves in your presence. Well newsflash, mister. I was not flirting with you, and what you saw there was my crazy daughter who is going through some insane teenage crisis where she wants to mortify her mother at every turn. Since you obviously can't understand that and feel the need to feed your ego at my expense, I suggest you and your pride turn around and leave, and don't let the door slam you in the back on the way out. You know what? On second thought, go ahead. Your pride could use a few bruises."

"I—" He was usually quick on the draw with responses, his job demanded that of him. But right now, he had no words. Part of him was flattered that she thought he had a "sexy physique and wildly handsome face" but just the fact that he felt that way proved her point. "You're right. I'll leave. Have a nice day."

He turned toward the door but his foot caught and his balance shifted. Reaching out a hand, he grabbed the first thing he touched, but a moment too late, he realized his mistake as the prickly branch gave way, and he went crashing to the ground. The sound of glass shattering echoed through the store, followed by a hush.

He opened his eyes. Beneath him was the large Christmas tree that had once stood in the middle of the shop, most of its ornaments in ruins.

And above him was a fire-breathing dragon dressed in a red apron with *Sadie* embroidered on the front.

2

"**G**et. Out. Of. My. Store.**" Sadie thrust the words at the man who had just single-handedly ruined this season's center piece display. The looking-uglier-by-the-minute stranger lay on her tree, broken ornaments surrounding him as if he'd pretended the glass was snow and tried to make a snow angel.

Mari stood behind him, her eyes wide and hands covering her mouth.

This was partially her fault, and as soon as Sadie figured out how to fix this mess, she would have a little heart-to-heart with her daughter. Yelling would most definitely be involved.

He struggled to get up and winced when he put his hand over a piece of glass. "You know, most store owners would be worried about liability and getting sued right about now instead of scowling at the customer."

Oh no he didn't. She gripped the shepherd still in her hand, resisting the urge to fling it at the man. "I can't believe you have the audacity to—"

Pushing to his feet, he shook glass off his coat. "Relax. I'm not suing you. Just pointing out a fact. To prove it, let me go back to my hotel and get my checkbook and I'll—"

A (kinda) Country Christmas

Why did rich guys think they could fix everything with a little wiggle of their pen and a few extra zeroes? "I don't want your money. I really just want you to leave." She couldn't think with him standing there, and *real* customers would be pouring in soon.

Mari stepped forward. "Mom, maybe you should—"

Sadie silenced her with a look. *The look* didn't work very well these days, but today Mari nodded her head and shut her mouth.

The man shook his head and raised his hands. "Sorry. I'll just leave then."

A shard of guilt pricked her chest when she saw the bloody nicks on his palm. But he wordlessly turned and left the shop, leaving behind the jingling door bell, a broken Christmas tree, and a pile of glass.

Sadie took a breath. "Well."

Mari tucked her hair behind her ears. "I guess we should clean up, huh."

Sadie only nodded, words stuck in her throat. This was *not* how she'd expected this day to start. Her last Christmas season with Mari by her side. Next year she'd be off to college, and Sadie would have to hire yet another stranger to help her.

What a depressing thought.

Flipping the sign back to the cursive *Closed,* Sadie grabbing a broom, handed it to Mari and carefully bent to pick up the tree. Branches were snapped in two and the base was bent. The *very* expensive artificial tree was not salvageable.

Wordlessly they worked, clearing the mess until there was just an empty circle in the middle of the store. A boring, unattractive bare circle.

Staring at the space, Mari fiddled with a strand of her hair. "I'm sorry, Mom."

The lecture she'd planned fizzled. "I forgive you. And I'm sorry too."

Mari looked up and met her eyes, her lips curled into a

smile. "You should have let the bald hottie write you a check."

"I know, right? I thought the same thing with every price tag I threw in the trash. Sometimes even mothers can make stupid decisions." Mari opened her mouth, but Sadie shook her head and winked. "No comments needed. But—hold on. Why do you think the man is bald? He never even took off his hat."

Her daughter shrugged. "Just a hunch. Plus, I can see you dating a bald guy. It would totally fit you."

"Oh good grief. I'm not dating anyone, bald or otherwise." Although bald would be a pretty opposite choice from her first love. Mari's father, Phin, used to have long hair, pulled perpetually back in a ponytail except for the occasional dreads. Every once in a while she wondered what ever came of him, but she tossed the thought away as quickly as it sprouted. "Now, will you go get that spare tree we keep in the back? We can go ahead and open the store and start redecorating. You're in charge of that, okay?"

"Sure."

"And Mari?"

"Yes?"

"Go crazy with the red and green, okay? You're in charge. Make it shine."

Her daughter smiled brighter than she had in ages and all but danced into the backroom.

Watching her leave, Sadie sighed, her heart surprisingly light again. Evidently the way to her daughter's heart was as easy as letting her decorate a Christmas tree.

Walking to the door, she flipped the sign back to open. The door handle caught her eye.

A splatter of blood dotted the metal.

She frowned. He must be in a lot of pain. Her own mother would jump out of her grave and give Sadie a stern talking to for being so mean to a customer.

And, the customer was right. He probably *could* sue her. Not that he'd get much out of her. The store barely kept them afloat each year, and with a loss as big as the one that had just shattered across the hardwood floor, it was yet another obstacle in her goal to help Mari pay for college next year.

Grabbing an antibacterial wipe from behind the cash register, she cleaned the handle and looked outside at the growing number of people milling down the street.

Had he mentioned what hotel he was at? No, she didn't think so, so calling and checking on him was not an option.

For that matter, she didn't even know his name.

Walking back to the little nativity, she arranged the figurines again, putting the shepherd back in his spot. Picking up baby Jesus, she sighed. God was probably shaking his head at her too. *Lord, I know I screwed this up. I was mean to a stranger instead of showing compassion. Some Christian I am. Forgive me. And help Mr. I-have-no-clue-his-name get better quickly.*

She conveniently didn't ask to bring him back so she could make amends.

If life had taught her anything, it was that sometimes the past was best left where it was.

3

N ate sucked in a breath as he plucked the last of the glass out of his left hand, swallowing the choice words that threatened to string off his tongue.

Old habits died hard.

He grabbed the antibiotic cream he'd gotten from the pharmacy on his walk back to the hotel and applied it liberally to the tiny cuts, then wrapped his hand in a bandage. Probably an overkill, but it was either that or about twelve Band-aids crisscrossing his palm.

Thankfully his right hand had landed in a fairly clear spot, and his coat had taken the brunt of the glass when he landed. He'd have to buy a new one, though, as his was covered in more glass than he had the patience to get out. And even if he did, it would probably fall apart from all the tiny holes.

But no, he wouldn't sue the woman. He was the idiot who had tripped up with both his mouth and his feet.

He wished she would have let him pay her for damages. He'd peeked at the tag on one of those glass ornaments. The price had made his eyes widen, and he doubted if even one had survived the fall.

A (kinda) Country Christmas

But he was banished from her store, and if God was the merciful creator he said he was, Nate would never have to see the woman again.

Maybe Kendra would take one look at his hand and ditch her crazy matchmaking plans. She'd been filling his phone with text messages about various single friends she thought would be perfect for him ever since he agreed to come this weekend to see her show. His little sister had gotten a gig at a theater in Pigeon Forge last year and had been on his case about coming to see her perform ever since. Work had always been in the way, but he'd let it slip last month that he would be home from China by Thanksgiving, so she'd roped him into it.

He'd actually been excited about the trip until the matchmaking texts began.

It wasn't that he didn't like women. On the contrary, not too many years ago, he'd rarely been seen outside of work without some woman on his arm. But it had all been superficial. He rarely dated them twice, and a few times they'd ended up in his bed at the end of the night. Basically, he'd been exactly the man that Sadie the Christmas store lady had accused him of being.

But that was the old Nate. God had brought him to his knees and used tragedy to slap a wet rag in his face and make him see what a broken man he'd become.

Despite what his earthly father had taught him, his Heavenly Father was in the business of taking broken, even despicable men and redeeming them.

He was living proof of that.

No. Liking women wasn't the problem. It was being worthy of one that was the snag. That, and the fact that most women who found out his past wanted nothing to do with his future.

Thankfully, Kendra was proving to be too busy with her job to be able to do the whole tour guide thing, much less introduce him to her "friends."

He'd go see her show tonight, grab breakfast with her

in the morning, then set his GPS to Hilton Head. He'd been anticipating more free time this winter, so he had kept his vacation house empty of renters just in case.

Now would be the perfect time to go. He had no trips scheduled until after the first of the year, and all his work could be done remotely. He could use some stress-free relaxation, and he planned to have just that this December.

But first, he needed to buy a new coat before he headed into Pigeon Forge for Kendra's show. He should have just stayed there, but she rented a place with a roommate here in Gatlinburg, so he'd wanted to be closer to her.

As he picked up his hotel keycard, his phone vibrated in his pocket. He fished it out to see Kendra's smiling face on the screen. She looked exactly how he remembered their mother. High cheekbones, extra lipstick, brown curls bursting from around her face, and a sparkle in her eye that shouted mischief.

He stuffed back the memory of their on-again-off-again mother and answered the phone. "Hey, sis. What's up?"

"Well, good and bad news. Which one you want to hear first?"

"Good. I've had enough bad myself today."

"Oh no. What did you do this time?"

The little imp. Always assuming the worse. "Nothing. Just—hurt my hand. So what's going on?"

"Well, the good news is that I get to spend more time with you."

He frowned. Not that he didn't love his sister, but if that was the good news then— "What's the bad news?"

"There was a small electrical fire at the theater. No big deal, but they're canceling tonight's show and adding an extra one tomorrow. I already exchanged your ticket for the show tomorrow. I know you were planning on leaving after breakfast, but you just *have* to come, Nate. You promised, remember?"

He'd made a bad habit of promising his little sister way too many things in his life, partially because their parents were too busy breaking promises and he felt it was his brotherly duty to fill in and make sure her dreams stayed intact. And then they were gone— and she had become his responsibility.

Sighing, he plopped onto the king-sized bed and fell back, letting the pillow-top cushion his fall. "Of course I'll come. I suppose this means we can do dinner tonight? Name the place and I'll meet you. My treat of course."

"Actually, I had a better idea. My roommate will be out late tonight, so I thought you could come over and I'd cook for you, just like old times."

His sister was a phenomenal cook. He'd tried to get her to go to culinary school, a slightly more lucrative career path than her major in dramatic arts and music. But she would hear none of it. "That sounds good. Do you have plans this afternoon, or what time do you want me there?"

"Unfortunately I still have to be there at the theater this afternoon for a few hours, but I'll see you at my house about six, that okay? I could arrange for you a tour guide this afternoon if you'd like. Oh, my friend—"

"No. Thank you though. I'll do just fine on my own."

"You sure?"

"Positive." An encounter with another single, non-related woman was the last thing he needed today.

4

"I'm so glad you could make it for dinner on such short notice. I wasn't sure if the shop would be too busy."

Sadie chopped the cucumbers for the salad and shrugged. The phone call from Kendra had come at the exact right time. Her friend's little cabin up on a mountain was the perfect place to relax for a few hours, complete with all the rustic decor, deer head on the mantle and all. Well, she could have done without the dead animal staring at her, but it was still a far cry from the small townhouse she and Mari shared just off the Parkway.

The short evening reprieve was needed tonight more than ever, since Mari had started in with her attitude again this afternoon, a smirk on her face after each customer compliment on the red, rustic themed tree she'd decorated.

Sadie had to hand it to her. She'd done a great job. The tree with its homemade red ornaments, all made by a local mom who created them out of her home, looked amazing. The ornaments were selling like hotcakes. It would barely make a dent in the loss of the original tree, but something was better than nothing. "It's been a long day. Mari had it under control, and I'd already scheduled Carla to work anyway."

"How is Carla working out? I was so proud of you finally hiring extra help. You can't do it all yourself, friend."

"Carla is a God-send. It's a win-win. I get a few evenings off, and she gets a part-time job that doesn't interfere with her day job to save up money for a new car." Sadie had even been able to start leading the kid's program at church on Wednesday nights again. It'd crushed her to give it up, but after Mom and Dad died, she'd had no choice.

"Well, I'm a social butterfly and keep a steady supply of friends looking for extra work, so if you ever need someone else, just say the word."

"Speaking of, you set the table for three. Who else is coming tonight?"

Kendra glanced at the table, eyebrows raised a little too innocently and replied, "Oh. That's for my brother. Did I forget to mention he's in town?"

Her relaxing evening took a nosedive toward a crash landing. "Kendra Meyers. Are you matchmaking again?"

Her hand fluttered to her chest. "Who me? I'd never do such a thing."

"I don't know why they hired you for an acting gig when you clearly have no skills at drama at all. We've talked about this before. I'm not interested. I already have everything I need and plenty to keep me busy. Mari and the shop are my life. I don't have time for anything else. Plus, I don't know of any man who would want to be saddled with a woman who celebrates Christmas three-hundred-sixty-five days a year."

Kendra crossed her arms over her chest and leaned a slim hip against the counter. "Maybe Nate isn't the guy for you. But as your friend, it's my responsibility to point out the fact that you can't keep hiding behind your daughter and that shop the rest of your life. Mari is leaving, and the shop—well. Look me in the eye and tell me you want to run the boutique all by yourself for the rest of your life."

"I—" Sadie scooped up the cucumbers and dumped them into the waiting bowl of spinach leaves. "—don't want to talk about this right now." Mostly because she didn't want to *think* about it. The rest of her life was a long time, while her time left with Mari was growing short. In fact, only their low bank account had kept her home an extra year.

The disquiet that had nibbled at her the last few months now screamed louder than a bullhorn.

"That's fine. I'm here to talk when you're ready. But for now, you get to meet the man who made me who I am today. My big brother in shining armor."

To hear Kendra talk, her brother hung the moon and stars and kept them all spinning with his pinkie. She hadn't said exactly his profession, but it was something nerdy like computers, and since his little sister had to resort to begging women to date him, he was probably—uh—yeah. She couldn't think of a nice way to put it. The man was probably uglier than a toad. But if he had a good heart, that was all that mattered. She wasn't interested in dating anyone anyway, so it would be someone else's problem. "I'm sure he's great."

The doorbell rang. Kendra swooped up the salad bowl and laid it on the small kitchen table. "Can you get the lasagna out of the oven while I go get Nate?"

"Sure."

Grabbing potholders out of the drawer, she slid a lasagna large enough to feed an army out of the oven and set it on top. Peeking under the foil, she inhaled. Ah yes. This is why she'd so readily accepted Kendra's invitation. Not only was the girl good for her heart, her cooking was good for the soul.

Voices jarred the silence of the mountain retreat, Kendra's as well as one low and masculine, and—a little familiar?

A (kinda) Country Christmas

Where had she heard—

The hunger pains in her stomach turned to churning. Oh no.

No. No. No. No. No.

She turned just in time see the handsome businessman, complete with a bandaged hand, pull off his stocking cap to reveal a perfectly shaped bald head.

5

Nate clutched his hat in his fist as he stared dumbfounded at Kendra's "friend" aka Sadie the shopkeeper. "What are you doing here?"

Her eyebrows arched high, hiding beneath those blond bangs of hers. "I was just getting ready to ask you the same thing."

Kendra folded her arms across her chest and glanced between them. "Can someone tell me what's going on here? How do you two know each other?"

Sadie didn't say a word, only spun back around to the pan on the stove.

Pretending as if her presence hadn't both irritated and intrigued him, Nate shrugged off his new coat and pretended that nothing was weird about this situation. "I was in her shop today."

Kendra still frowned. "You went to Bethlehem's Boutique? Okay, that makes sense. But why are you two acting—"

He raised his bandaged hand. "There was a little accident."

Her eyes widened. "You said you hurt your hand but—

A (kinda) Country Christmas

I didn't realize it was bad. What'd you do, break something with your hand?"

Sadie glanced over her shoulder and shot him a withering look. "He broke a lot of somethings."

Kendra jabbed her hands on her hips, looking back and forth between Nate and Sadie. "Why am I just finding out about this?"

"Because I didn't know she was your friend and didn't think it mattered."

Sadie set the lasagna down onto the table with a thud. "And I had no idea he was your brother."

Kendra ran a hand through her dark brown curls and tucked them behind her ear. "Let me get this straight. Sadie, Nate went to your store this morning and broke some stuff, hurting his hand in the process. While that stinks, I'm sure it was an accident. Why do I get the feeling you both want to strangle each other?"

Nate moved to shove his hands into his pockets but remembered too late that his left hand wouldn't fit with its bandage so let it dangle at his side. "I wouldn't say we want to strangle each other."

Sadie looked up and caught his eye, a humorous spark coming from her gaze. "Although someone did threaten to sue..."

Kendra gaped at him. "Nate, you didn't."

"You're right. I *didn't*." He pierced Sadie with his gaze. Clearly Kendra's friend was a troublemaker. "I told her that I could sue her, but wouldn't. I even offered to pay her for the damages, which she refused."

Kendra turned back Sadie. "Is that true?"

"Well, technically. But—it was my tree, Kendra. The Christmas centerpiece for this year. He fell into it. All the ornaments are a loss."

His sister's mouth turned to a perfect O. "Oh my goodness. No. That tree was my favorite! And those ornaments were—"

Sadie sighed and fiddled with the foil that covered the

pan. "Expensive."

Nate felt a bucket of remorse pour over him. He really should pay for it. "My offer still stands. I have no problem—"

She shook her head. "No. You were right. It is the cost of doing business. We'll figure it out."

He wasn't a math genius, but he was pretty business savvy. The tree itself had to cost a pretty penny, and there had to be over a hundred of those costly glass ornaments. Even if her little store was a success, she wasn't raking in the kind of dough that she could take a hit like that. He, on the other hand, could take the hit even with a few extra zeros at the end. "I'm a clumsy mess. Kendra will tell you. Really, I want to help."

His sister coughed to the side, then nodded. "He's right. The man couldn't walk a straight line even if there was a million dollars at the end of it. And he's loaded. He can afford it."

Leave it to Kendra. But at least she'd kept up the fib for him. If there was anyone who was clumsy, it was his sister.

Sadie eyed them both then shook her head. "Let's not talk about this now. Supper is getting cold."

Dinner was eaten mostly in silence, Kendra trying her best to draw Nate and Sadie out but failing miserably.

As the two women stood to clear the table, Nate caught sight of the swirling white outside the kitchen window. "Kendy, did you know it was supposed to snow?"

Her gaze snapped to the window. "No. I didn't. Can you check the weather real quick? It's probably just a little front coming through."

Tapping his phone's screen, he opened his weather app and frowned at the red warning across the top, then scrolled down to the radar. "Well, that's not good. There's a blizzard warning out. Looks like it was supposed to go north of us but shifted direction. It's just starting but they're calling for a foot or more by morning."

Kendra frowned. "Well that bites. You guys should

probably head down the mountain then."

"You okay up here by yourself? What about the show tomorrow?"

"If it's too bad, they'll cancel. But I'll be fine. I survived last winter by myself, remember? And every other winter for the last eight years."

He tugged on one of her curls like he used to do when she was little. "Just lookin' out for you, Squirt."

She pushed him. "You know I hate that name. Now scat." She glanced over at Sadie who was busy filling the dishwasher. "You too, girl."

"Hey, I've lived here longer than you. A little snow doesn't scare me."

"It's not just a little. Did you not hear the word *blizzard?*"

Sadie put in the last plate and turned around, wiping her hands on a dishrag. "I know, I know. I want to get back for Mari anyway."

"Good. You two get ready to go, I'm going to run upstairs and get you some blankets to put in your cars just in case."

Nate pulled on his hat and coat as he watched Sadie outfit herself for the weather as well, complete with a puffy, red winter jacket that resembled a marshmallow, a hat with a little poof on the top, and knitted gloves covered in green and red chevron stripes. She leaned over to tug on her brown, fur-topped boots, giving him a very nice but inappropriate view of her jean-hugged backside.

"You have a problem with something?"

He snapped his gaze up to see she'd glanced over at him. "Nope. Just admiring your—hat. Very cute." Yeah. Her hat. That was it. *Behave, Nate. Eyes up.*

She scowled but bent down, thankfully at her knees this time, and finished securing her boots.

When she stood back up, she glanced over him, her gaze moving down to his toes then back up to his eyes. If he hadn't known better, he would have guessed she was checking him out or something.

"Is that all you're wearing out there?"

He looked down to his black coat. It was the warmest one he could find that didn't make him look like puff the magic marshmallow. "Yeah, why?"

"No gloves?"

"I'm not used to the snow. Bought the hat at the airport when I got in yesterday." He turned his head either way. "Spiffy, huh?"

The roll of her eyes said her opinion before her words did. "You seem to have a color palette of one going on. Black coat. Black hat. Robbing a bank soon or something?"

"I prefer to earn my money, thank you very much. And my shirt is blue. I like to mix it up occasionally."

Her mouth tipped into—was that a smile? "Well, I stand corrected. You are obviously the paragon of chic and stylish."

He started to retort but Kendra came down the stairs, arms laden with quilts. "I have two for each of you. Never can be too careful."

Nate grabbed the quilts off the top, not caring that they were way too girly for his taste, and squeezed his sister in a sideways bear hug. "Be safe, okay?"

She hugged him back. "Of course. Aren't I always?"

If only. "Don't make me start a list—"

Pushing him toward the door, she laughed. "Okay, okay. I'll be safe. *You* be safe driving. It's really coming down out there. You sure you don't want to crash on the couch?"

With the possibility of being snowed in for a few days? "Thanks, but I really need to get back to the hotel and finish up a few work things tonight."

Kendra huffed. "Maybe it's a good thing my matchmaking scheme failed, Sadie. This one is obviously a workaholic."

Sadie grabbed her quilts and hugged her friend as well.

A (kinda) Country Christmas

"See? All things work out for the best."

Nate opened the door, letting in a *whoosh* of frigid air and white flakes. Sadie followed on his heels and headed for her ancient Ford pickup. Not what he would have expected from the woman who looked more like a twelve-year-old in her winter attire, but he supposed it was good in the weather.

Getting in his own rented Expedition, he cranked the engine and turned the heat on high. Rubbing his hands to gain some warmth, he glanced over at Sadie's truck. The old clunker revved to life, but after a few moments, a chug and a few gasps echoed across the drive, followed by silence.

6

Sadie beat the steering wheel with her gloved fist then rested her forehead against it.

Why now?

The truck had been on its last legs for close to ten years, but Dad had always kept it kicking.

But now, she wasn't sure there was any mechanical CPR that could cure the noises that had just clanked from the engine before it went silent.

A tapping rapped on her window, and she jerked her head up to see Nate standing beside the truck, shivering, his arms wrapped around his body. He shouted through the glass, "Need a jump?"

She didn't know a lot about cars, but she knew a jump wouldn't come close to curing what ailed the old darlin'. Jerking out the keys, she grabbed her purse and hopped down from the cab, gritting her teeth against the cold. "It's done for. I'll need to get it towed."

"You live in Gatlinburg?"

She nodded, fearing that he would offer her a lift and knowing she'd have no choice but to accept.

"My hotel is right on the parkway. I can give you a lift."

A (kinda) Country Christmas

"Thanks. I appreciate it. You get back in so you don't freeze to death. I'll run and go tell Kendra."

After a quick promise to her friend to call for a tow as soon as the weather cleared, Sadie ran back to Nate's SUV, barely controlling the urge to give the old truck a swift kick in the tire for betraying her.

Shutting the door behind her, she tugged off her gloves and warmed her hands in the vents. "Thank you for the lift. I really appreciate it."

"No problem." Nate pulled out of the driveway and slowly started the descent down the winding mountain road. "How old is that truck anyway?"

"Too old. 1970 Ford. My dad's pride and joy."

"Wow. Think it's fixable?"

Sadie shrugged. "No clue. Dad always took care of it."

He glanced over at her. "Is your dad—"

An emptiness she tried to ignore tugged at her. "He died a few years ago of a heart attack, shortly after Mom. She died of cancer. I've always thought his heart just kinda broke after losing her and couldn't take it anymore."

He glanced at her. "I'm sorry for your loss."

A nice, polite response. Loss was putting it mildly. Her parents had been a little odd, she would admit. Okay, maybe a *lot* odd. But they had loved big and had gone home close to each other, which had always been their prayer. "Thank you. But let me suggest you keep your eyes on the road." She frowned at the snow pelting the windshield. "It's getting worse. I'm sorry, I should have offered to drive."

His smile was big but his white knuckles on the steering wheel told the story. "I'm a big boy. I can drive in snow."

"Aren't you used to private jets and limos or something?"

He laughed, a nice, deep throaty sound that a girl could get used to hearing. Not this girl, though. "I think Kendra must have exaggerated a little. I don't own nor could I afford a private jet, and I'm a big fan of rental cars, not rental drivers. I have even mastered driving on the opposite side of the road and car in a few countries. Want me to demonstrate?"

She sat up quickly. "Don't you dare."

A chuckle rumbled from his chest. "Relax. It was a joke. You know what those are, right?"

Sitting back, she blew out a shaky breath. "Sorry. I'm usually not this crazy. The weather's frazzling my nerves." She just wanted to get home to her little townhouse, make sure Mari was safe and sound and warm, run a nice, hot bubble bath, and melt the bad day away.

Pulling out her cell, she tapped a message to Mari, making sure she had made it home from the shop okay. She watched but the cell gave a warning message about no service available.

Just great.

A few minutes later, Sadie squinted at something odd at the side of the road. What was— "Deer!"

Nate slammed on the brakes, the anti-lock brakes kicking into gear and jerking them to a stop, as the buck darted in front of them.

They skidded to a stop, just narrowly missing the tail end of the animal.

Her heart jammed into her chest as she tried to process what had almost happened. Were they in the twilight zone today or something? She would ask what else could go wrong but feared it might usher in a freak December tornado or something.

Nate reached across and grabbed her hand. His solid grip comforted her more than it should, but right now, she didn't care. "Are you okay?"

She nodded. "I think my heart has resumed beating again. You?"

"I'm alright. You ready to keep going? It's only a few more miles I think."

"Yes. I need to get home and check on Mari. Just hope we make it in one piece."

"You and me both."

They made it to the parkway without incident. The road was oddly quiet for this time of night, only a few brave souls illuminated by the brilliant Christmas lights that lined the road and hung off each building. Sadie directed him to her little townhouse complex a few blocks off the main drag. He pulled into a parking spot in front of the unit she pointed out. "Well, we made it. One piece."

She tucked her hair behind her ear and tugged on her hat again. "A true Christmas miracle in this weather. I don't envy your drive up the parkway, but at least you're close."

Nate cleared his throat. "Listen, before I go—about the store. I want to—"

"No, really, please don't worry about it." Her gaze dipped to his bandaged hand. Her fault. "I'm sorry about your hand. I should have—"

He plucked a piece of paper out of a cup holder between them, took her hand, and pressed it into her palm. "I insist. I was clumsy. It was my mistake. Please let me help make it right. It'll ruin my Christmas if I don't do something to make up for it."

She glanced down to where he still held her hand with both of his. His warm skin was like a hot compress, dulling her good senses. She really shouldn't take it... "Okay. Thank you."

With a final squeeze, he released her hand and smiled, displaying that adorable dimple he probably despised but every woman loved. "You're welcome, and again, I'm sorry."

Stuffing the check into her pocket, she tugged her gloves on and grabbed her purse. "Well, I know you're leaving soon, so I probably won't see you. But it was nice meeting you. Have a safe trip."

He shook his head. "Liar-liar. It wasn't nice meeting me, and you know it."

A few hours ago, Sadie would have agreed with him.

But there was something intriguing about her friend's brother. But it didn't matter. She'd probably never see him again, and that was definitely for the best. "Just remember, you said it, not me." She retorted back with a laugh as she opened the door and slid down to the snow-packed pavement.

Shutting the door behind her, she trekked up the sidewalk to the end-unit townhouse she shared with her daughter.

Turning to wave, she kept her hand down as the SUV lumbered out of the parking lot.

A pang of regret stung her, but she shook her head. It was for the best.

Hurrying inside, she tried not to shiver as she peeled off her damp coat and gloves and kicked off her boots. "Mari, you home?"

"Kitchen."

Padding down the hall, she breathed in the heavenly scent of cookies baking that just started to fill the room. "Cooking?"

Her daughter was rolling out dough on the counter, a poof of flour dotting her cheek. "It's cold. It's the first weekend of December. I figured now was a good time."

"Want some help?"

Her daughter eyed her like she'd just suggested they rob a bank together. "What do you think?"

It was a well-known fact that Sadie couldn't bake if her life depended on it. She managed most meals okay, just not to Kendra's culinary genius level. But baking—not-so-much. She'd ruined every baked good she'd ever attempted, from birthday cakes to brownies to the most sad thing of all, Christmas cookies.

There wasn't a lot more pathetic than a crispy Santa-shaped sugar cookie.

Still, it always made her sad not to help with the Christmas cookies. "Well, how about I frost when you're done?"

A (kinda) Country Christmas

"On one condition."

Sadie sat at a bar stool and frowned. "Hey, who's mother and who's daughter here?"

Mari tucked a blond curl behind her ear and shot her a smile. "Do you want to help or not?"

"Fine. What's your condition?" She'd frost the cookies regardless. But she might as well humor the girl.

"You tell me all about your date with Mr. Hottie out there."

Oh crud. She'd hoped Mari hadn't seen him. "First, he has a name. Nate Meyers. Turns out our tree-wrecker is Kendra's big brother."

Mari paused mid-roll and gawked. "No way."

"Yes way. And unlucky for me, he came into town this weekend and Kendra just *happened* to invite me to dinner, and conveniently left out that it was dinner for three."

"Wow. So, how did that go?"

"About as bad as you could imagine, although the lasagna was to die for." She reached for her over-sized purse she'd set on the floor and grabbed the container from it. "Kendra sent you leftovers."

"Thanks, but don't change the subject. How did this dinner-date go from bad to him escorting you home?"

"Truck died. For good I think. I've never heard such awful noises come from an engine before."

Mari set aside the rolling pin and leaned against the counter, worry beyond her years etched in her eyes. "What are we going to do? We need that to—"

She held up a hand to stop her. "It's my concern. Not yours. Let Momma worry about it, okay?"

"Fine. But back to my original question. Could there, like, be something between you and this Nate guy?"

Oh good grief. Her daughter, the hopeless romantic. "No. Definitely not. He's too—urban."

Mari wrinkled her nose. "What, like, Keith?"

"Huh? Who's Keith?" Then it clicked. Crazy child. "No. You and your country music. I mean urban as in city-boy. He travels the world, owns a vacation house on the beach, grew up in New York City. He wouldn't be interested in a country bumpkin like me."

"You're not as country as you think you are, Mom."

She'd lived in the epitome of country for almost twenty years. Of course she was. "Mari, I—"

"No, listen Mom. You lived here because Grandma and Grandpa moved here, and you wanted their help to raise me. I get it. But this was never *your* home. You don't act like a country girl. Just like that crazy tree you decorated in the shop. That should have been on display in some fancy New York City Christmas display, not here. Gatlinburg is more burlap and bows than glass and sparkle."

The girl had no idea what she was talking about. "I fit in here just fine. Do I need to go get my cowgirl boots and hat to prove it?"

Mari slid a pan of cookies out of the oven and plopped it down on the oven. "What is that Shakespeare quote you're always spouting off to me? Methinks you protest too much?"

"If you're going to quote him, get it right, dear. It's 'The lady doth protest too much, methinks.'"

"Whatever. You know what I meant."

She did, and she also didn't want to discuss it, especially with her daughter. Her inner struggles about where she belonged were not something she had let anyone in on, and she wasn't about to start today. "Well, in other news, Mr. Urban Hottie gave us a check to help with the tree."

Her daughter's eyebrows shot up. "Really?"

Sadie pulled the check from her pocket and set it, still folded, on the counter. "It probably won't even cover the cost of that tree, but it'll help some." Maybe they could get a loan from the bank for a used car to replace the truck.

It'd be tight, but they would figure it out.

"I have a little saved from my paychecks if it would help."

"Absolutely not. You need to be saving for college,

remember? That was the plan."

Mari slid the cup of homemade frosting over to Sadie and a tray of un-iced cookies. "So, how much is it?"

Sadie picked up the first cookie and started to slather the green mixture over it. "I haven't even looked at it yet."

Before Sadie could argue, Mari snatched up the check and turned it over. She paused, then her throat bobbed as if she was swallowing something thick.

"Mom—"

Sadie cringed. It probably wouldn't even cover the cost of the artificial tree. "It's okay, we can always—"

"No. Mom, look."

Mari turned the check toward her.

The cookie in Sadie's hand plummeted to the floor.

7

Nate stood at the hotel window, amazed at how the scene below had transformed overnight.

Gone were the patchy bits of snow here and there, and in their place rested a fresh blanket of white as if God himself had doused the town with a bit of powdered sugar in celebration of Jesus' birth.

The plows had already been through, so the streets were mostly clear and the sidewalks seemed walkable between fresh mounds of snow. They'd ended up getting only half the snowfall that had been predicted.

Kendra had already called to cancel breakfast. The show was still on for this afternoon but she had to be there early and wasn't going to be able to make it to Gatlinburg beforehand.

Which left him in a quandary.

Usually he could easily fill his time with work, but it was Sunday, and that didn't sound appealing in the least.

He could always find a church—

He'd suggested it to Kendra originally, but she'd only laughed. It concerned him, but then he reminded himself that he would have done the same thing five years ago.

A (kinda) Country Christmas

But now that he was free for the morning, he had no excuse.

Grabbing his laptop, he flopped onto the bed and did a quick search of nearby churches.

As the page loaded, a knock rapped on the door.

He frowned. Must have forgotten to put the DO NOT DISTURB card in the key slot for housekeeping.

Flipping open the deadbolt, he opened the door a crack, mindful of his bare chest and sleep pants. "I'm sorry, I don't need—"

Words died in his throat at the sight of Sadie standing there, arms folded, fire blazing in her eyes.

"Sadie, I—"

She pushed the door open and charged past him. Her hair was thrown up in a sloppy ponytail, her bangs straight and twitching every which way instead of their normal, manicured curl right at her eyebrows. "Care to explain this?" In her outstretched hand was the check he'd scrawled out last night while she'd gone back in to tell Kendra about her broken down truck.

He'd started to write it out for a grand, but then he'd looked at her truck in all its rundown glory. It was as if his fingers acted with a mind of their own as they added another zero, scribbled the *ten thousand dollars and 0/100* in barely readable cursive, and signed it.

A peace had settled over him as he tucked the check away to give to her later.

But to explain that to her? He'd assumed she would be grateful and that he would never hear from her again, except maybe a thank you through Kendra. "I wanted to repay—"

"You and I both know the damage done in the store wasn't anywhere close to ten thousand dollars. I don't know what kind of—"

"Sadie."

"—Game you're trying to play here but—"

He interrupted her again, louder this time. "Sadie."

She huffed and crossed her arms across her chest. "What?"

"Do you believe in God?" His next words would depend on her answer.

Suspicion never left her eyes, but the anger lines softened a bit. "Yes. I do. Why?"

"So you're a Christian?"

Her eyes widened a bit in curiosity. "Yes. Not always a very good one, but I am."

Nate turned to the counter above the mini-fridge and poured himself a cup of coffee he'd had brewing, anything to keep his mind on task and off the fact that he was alone with a beautiful woman in his hotel room, and he was wearing only flannel pajama pants. He'd pull on a shirt but was afraid it'd just draw attention to a place her thoughts hadn't even gone. His, however, were a different story. "You and I both know there is no good or bad Christian. We're all saved by grace from the same God." He and his wayward thoughts were in need of that grace right now. He picked up the extra disposable cup. "Coffee?"

She eyed the cup, hesitating, but shook her head. "No. And we're getting off the subject. What does this all have to do with the money?"

Pouring her a cup anyway, he handed it to her. She accepted it as he figured she would. Two cups of hot liquid between them as a barrier was a *very* good thing. "Because God told me to add a zero to the check. "

She sipped out of the rim of the cup and glared at him. "He did not."

"Believe me, sweetheart. I don't go around throwing ten grand at women in distress just for kicks." The endearment slipped out before he could stop it. He just couldn't help it. She looked downright adorable when she was mad.

He regretted his slip even more when her eyes narrowed. "Sweetheart?"

Not being able to explain the—fine, he'd admit it—the

attraction he felt every time she was near, he chose to ignore her question. "Listen. Tear the check up if you want. But I honestly felt like it was the amount God was telling me to give. I was a jerk yesterday, and call it buying myself peace or whatever you want, it's what I needed to do."

She stared at him for longer than was appropriate before her gaze drifted to his shirtless torso. She quickly averted her eyes, looking everywhere but at him. "Okay. Fine. But for the record. I don't need your money or your pity."

"I never said you did." Although he had a sneaky feeling she *did* need a little money.

She turned to leave, but as her hand covered the doorknob, a horrible idea hit him, and the words popped out of his mouth before he could stop them. "Sadie, do you go to church?"

Oh why couldn't he just let her go?

She turned back around, and her stomach started with its crazy two-step again.

No man should look that amazing without a shirt on. It'd been way too long—and she felt way too weak this morning after a long night of tossing and turning, filled with crazy dreams that may or may not have starred the man standing in front of her.

She'd woken up for the last time at four a.m. and decided it was all his fault she couldn't sleep. He had looked at her as a charity case, which she most certainly was *not*, and she would fix that as soon as it was a respectable time to show up. She'd had to call Kendra and ask a few innocent sounding questions to get the name of his hotel. And thankfully the front desk clerk was a girl Mari had graduated high school with, so getting his room number had been simple.

Mari had told her she was out of her mind, to just take the money. But then, she was only eighteen. She couldn't begin to understand.

But truth was, Sadie didn't really understand it all either.

She looked at him again and his eyebrows were raised expectantly.

Oh, yeah.

Church. Yes, that'd been his question. She forced her eyes to meet his gaze, not even an inch lower. "Yes, I—usually go to church. But Mari and I are staying home this morning." No need to mention it was because they didn't have a way to get there, and while on a nice day she might have walked, today, after already walking here, not so much.

His eyes held a question, probably the *why aren't you going* one she refused to answer, so she continued. "I'd be happy to give you the address and directions though."

He handed her the hotel scratch pad and pen. "Thanks. Kendra canceled on me for breakfast, so I thought I'd try out a local church. The roads look clear enough."

She scribbled the address and a few quick directions onto the paper and handed it back. "Hope you enjoy it."

He followed her to the door. "Wait, you didn't walk all the way here, did you?"

Stepping into the hallway, she eyed the elevator then glanced back at him. "No, I flew. Didn't you know? Jet packs are all the rage these days."

"Now that I'd like to see. But seriously. It's like a mile up the parkway. You were that mad at me?"

Yes. That's what one does when a man causes her to have nightmares and little sleep. "I always go for a morning walk, I just directed it here is all." And added about a half-mile uphill to her normal walking routine and froze her booty off the whole way.

"If you hold on a minute, I can drive—"

She took a few backward steps. "No really. I'm good.

A (kinda) Country Christmas

Have a nice time at church." Turning, she fled to the elevator and jabbed the down button.

His low voice called out from where he stood in the doorway. "What time does church start?"

She glanced back as the elevator dinged. "Ten-forty-five."

"Good. I'll pick you and Mari up at ten-thirty. Be ready."

Before she could protest, he stepped back and let the hotel door slam closed in front of him.

8

Sadie slipped a long, green cable-knit sweater over her head and tugged it down over her jeans with a huff.

She should have knocked on that door again and told him not even to think about showing up at her house.

But she was a big, honkin' pushover. A people pleaser who had an insanely difficult time telling people, except for Mari, no.

And he said all the right words.

God told me to give you the money.

I'm taking you to church.

How does a good Christian woman say no to logic like that?

She doesn't. At least not this one.

And where was that *good Christian woman* when she was standing there, alone with him in a hotel room, staring at his well-chiseled chest and abs? Okay, there was a *little* pudge there, and he was no Channing Tatum or anything, but he obviously worked out and it looked good on him.

Blinking, she shook her head again to get the alluring image from her brain.

A (kinda) Country Christmas

Stop it, Sadie. She should not be ogling a man. It was physical attraction, plain and simple. And just like she taught her daughter, looking at a boy at skin level may please the eyes but was dangerous for the heart. It's the inside that counts.

And so far, Nate Meyers had shown himself to be pushy, overbearing, demanding, and controlling.

He was nothing like her. She was a country mouse, and he was a city lion. He'd swallow her whole.

So then, why was she getting ready to ride to church with him?

Because her traitor heart had gone all school-girl giddy at the idea of riding next to him.

Slipping on a pair of knee-high, brown leather boots over her jeans, she turned and surveyed herself in the full-length mirror.

Nothing fancy, but not too casual. Perfect for her laid back church. And the heels of the boots gave her a few extra inches in height so she'd be on Nate's level. He wasn't overly tall, maybe 5'10 if he were lucky, so the extra inches should work nicely.

Tucking her blond hair behind her ears, she frowned. It wasn't like she'd be standing next to him the whole time. They weren't going as a couple or anything.

Who was she kidding? Every member of her small church would be needling her with questions about the handsome man she brought to church. Wouldn't they be disappointed.

Grabbing a chunky beige scarf, she wrapped it around her neck, took one last look in the mirror, then headed downstairs.

Mari was already in the kitchen, sipping on a cup of coffee. "Wow, Mom. You look nice. Big date?"

Grabbing a mug, she poured herself her third cup of the day. She'd be bouncing off the walls by the time service started. "Shush. He's just taking us to church as a nice gesture, okay?"

"Whatever you say."

Sadie pierced her daughter with her gaze. "Mari, don't go there."

She fluttered her hand at her chest, looking all fake-innocent. "Go where, mother-dear? All I'm saying is that Kendra's hunky big brother seems to be awfully attentive to you."

"You sound like you *want* me to date him." The very idea was absurd.

"Maybe I do. What's so bad about that? You're smart, single. You deserve happiness too, Mom." Mari set her cup in the sink and turned around, her straightened blond hair framing her face beautifully. She looked so—grown up. When had that happened?

Pushing the thought away, she set down her cup and shook her head. "I have all the happiness I need, sweetie. I have an amazing daughter, a job where I get to celebrate the best holiday all year long, and a God who loves me. I can't get much more blessed than that." The words coming out of her mouth sounded really good. It was all true, right?

Then why did she feel like her joy had been sucked clear out of her?

It'd all started when—

The doorbell rang.

Sadie frowned. It'd all started when Nate Meyers stepped into her store yesterday.

Turning on her heel, she walked to the door, back straight, to greet Mr. Joy Stealer himself.

Standing with her hand on the knob, she took a breath. She could do this. She would go to church. Keep a nice, twelve-inch distance between them. Introduce him to all the eligible women in the church, and wash her hands of him.

He was leaving tomorrow anyway.

Then her joy could return in abundance.

A (kinda) Country Christmas

Nate rested his hand on the dip in Sadie's back, guiding her through the crowd that gathered after service in the small country church. It was quaint, complete with hymnals in the pews and stained glass windows lining the sanctuary—much different than some of the mega churches he'd attended in various cities across the globe.

Yet the church members were nothing like he'd expected. He'd dressed in a suit and tie, but they were all in jeans and sweaters, with a few dress slacks and skirts mixed in. He'd shaken more hands than he could count and declined over a dozen invitations for Sunday dinner.

The pastor, decked out in jeans, a dress shirt with buttons straining around his midsection, and cowboy boots, waved them over to where he stood. "Sadie. I see you brought a guest today."

She looked up at Nate, her cheeks tinged a light pink. "Yes. Pastor Silas, this is Nate Meyers. He's, uh, the brother of a friend of mine. He asked if I could recommend a good church, and of course I said I could. Then he—"

Nate squeezed her waist, cutting off her rambling, then reached out to shake the pastor's hand. "The message was great, Pastor. I really enjoyed it."

And that was the whole truth. It was about not letting our own desires and agendas override God's. All Nate could think about was driving to South Carolina tomorrow morning and how with every passing hour, it felt less and less right.

Was God trying to tell him something?

Yet staying in the mountains made no sense. He'd have to find a temporary place to stay, somewhere he had good Internet access so he could still work. And no doubt Kendra would be busy with her own job, so it wasn't like they'd get a lot of extra time together.

What was the point?

There wasn't one.

Pastor Silas flashed him a grin. "Glad to hear it, son. Will we see you back here next Sunday?"

Sadie shook her head with a little more force than necessary. "No, he's leaving tomorr—"

"Actually, maybe. I'm tossing around the idea of staying in town through Christmas." There. He'd said it. And now that the words had left his mouth, they sounded good.

Christmas in the mountains with his sister. Kendra would be ecstatic.

Sadie, however, looked up at him as if he'd just grown antlers. "You're what?"

He shrugged. "I can work remotely. Kendra's been begging me to spend Christmas with her for years. So why not? I'm usually stuck in some foreign country for work over the holidays, so this will be a treat."

The pastor's eyes lit up like a Christmas tree. "You travel for work, then?"

Nate nodded. "All over the globe. I'm a consultant in project management and specialize in companies that are struggling, helping them turn things around and put processes in place to keep them on track." He also helped close down companies that didn't stand a chance. That was the worst part of his job, like a corporate version of assisted suicide. He usually left that depressing detail out of his job description though.

Pastor Silas crossed his arms and put a hand to his chin, stroking his beard. "You know, Sadie, if Nate's going to be around a while, he could help us with the play."

If a record had been playing in Nate's head, it just let off an awful screech as it grinded to a stop. "Wait, what?" His sister was the thespian, not him.

Sadie was shaking her head and not liking whatever the pastor was talking about either. "I don't think that's such a good idea."

But Pastor Silas looked happier than a kid chomping on

A (kinda) Country Christmas

a peppermint stick. "Nonsense. Sadie here leads the kids every year in the annual Christmas play at church. They perform it during the Christmas Eve service. This year, the theme is Christmas around the globe, highlighting how different countries celebrate the birth of Christ. With your experience, you'd be the perfect person to help her."

Give him a failing billion dollar company, and he was in his comfort zone. Even throw in a dash of corporate espionage, and he'd sniff it out. A play? That'd be bad enough. But kids? No way. Not happening. Nate stuffed his sweaty palms into his pockets and shook his head. "I don't think—"

Sadie perked up and elbowed him in the side. "Actually, now that I think about it, it's a fabulous idea. Nate will be perfect, and I bet we can even find a fun part for him."

The evil pastor nodded. "You were just telling me last week you needed a Joseph."

"You're right. He would be perfect for the part!"

Nate waved a hand. "Hello. I'm still here, you know?"

Sadie patted his arm. "We know. Now, let's go chat about plans. Good talking with you, Pastor."

Pastor Silas grinned and waved as Sadie all but pushed him out of the sanctuary and down the front steps of the church.

Nate grabbed her arm and pulled her to the side away from the listening ears of the church members still loitering around. "What do you think you're doing?"

Sadie hiked her chin up a notch. "Payback."

"For what?"

"You know what." She lowered her voice, mimicking him. "*I'll be at your house at ten-thirty. Be ready.* Door slam. How was I supposed to say no to that?"

"So let me get this straight. I wanted to be nice and take you to church since you obviously didn't have a vehicle to drive, and this makes me a bad guy?"

"Nope. But it does make you a guy who is going to be helping out with a children's play at church."

"I'm not fond of—or rather, good with kids." Understatement of the year. Really, he'd never been around kids to know one way or the other. Truth be told, they scared him.

"Jesus said let the children come to me. They won't bite, Nate."

He shuddered. There was a chance the little rug-rats would bite?

But he'd already agreed. In front of the Pastor. He really didn't have another choice. "Fine. I'll help, but I will not, I repeat not, act in your little play as Joseph."

Sadie burst out laughing. "I'd forgotten about that. No worries. We were just joking. The part of Mary and Joseph have already been officially cast. No adults are allowed in the play anyway, per me."

Mari popped over beside Sadie, a silly grin on her face. "So Nate. I here you're staying for a while and helping Mom with the play."

He folded his arms and brooded. "Gossip much?"

She shrugged. "It's a small church. I overheard. All I can say is, watch out for Jacob. He's going through a biting stage and boy, the kid's got some sharp chompers."

9

The bell over the door at Bethlehem's Boutique jingled shortly after Sadie flipped the sign to OPEN. She looked up from the display of candy cane ornaments she was fixing to see Kendra, cheeks rosy from the cold, all but dance into the shop. "Did you hear?"

Sadie had been fearing this visit. "Be careful. I don't need another Meyers sibling downing a tree."

Dropping into the gold and red-velvet chair usually reserved for the once-a-week visit from Santa, Kendra crossed her legs at the knees and sat back, looking very queenish. "You did a really good job on the replacement, by the way. It looks amazing."

Glancing at the tree that stood at the center of the shop, Sadie smiled. "That was Mari's doing. She has a knack for design, and I'll admit, it fits in a lot better than my tree had. Hers is a classic country Christmas, definitely more Gatlinburg style. I'm constantly having to restock the tree with ornaments."

"You always did have a more modern, chic style."

Much to her parents irritation. Maybe that's why she'd been so adamant about that stupid tree. Last year was the first year without Mom and Dad at the store, and she'd gone out of her way to mimic what they would have done. But this year, she'd wanted to make it her own, add a little flare.

Turning the striped canes so they were all the same direction, Sadie sighed.

But what happened when her flare didn't fit her surroundings?

What happened when *she* didn't fit them?

Good grief. She was too young for an identity crisis. This was her life, and she liked it.

She just needed to do a better job at convincing her heart of that.

Kendra rapped her fingers against the arm of Santa's chair. "Hello? Earth to Sadie?"

Had she asked a question? "I'm sorry, I was—my brain's a thousand places today. What did you need?"

"Weren't you even a little curious as to my news I came bouncing in here to tell you?"

"Nate deciding to stay for Christmas, you mean?"

Kendra stomped her foot in toddler-like fashion. "He told you already?"

If Kendra didn't know that she knew, then she probably didn't know about the play either.

An idea formed.

Kendra hated the very mention of church. She'd laugh and change the subject every time Sadie said the word. But she loved her brother and loved everything to do with drama.

Maybe—

Sadie let the thought settle for a moment. Her friend had yet to attend church with her—but if it was a play— and for kids—and her brother was involved....

Yes, it might just work. "Yeah, he actually took Mari and me to church yesterday and told me then."

Kendra shifted in her seat. "Oh?"

"Mmmhmm. He's going to help me out with the

children's Christmas play."

Her friend sat up, jaw dropped. "He's what?"

"Our theme is Christmas around the globe, so we thought, what better person to help than a guy who's traveled the world, right?"

"But Nate doesn't know the slightest thing about acting or kids. He's—no. I promise you, he's a great big brother and all, but you do not want him around children."

Sadie bit her bottom lip. Maybe she should have thought this through more— "Is there something you need to tell me about your brother?"

Kendra popped up from the chair. "Oh my goodness, no. Nothing like, sinister or anything. Nate's a good guy. He's just never been overly fond of kids, and he hated the idea of me going into theater. So a church play for kids doesn't seem to be up his alley. However, if your finance team needs a few pointers, he'd be your guy."

"Well, that's good. I was starting to wonder just what kind of guy you were trying to set me up with."

Kendra grabbed an elf hat off a display and tried it on. She looked more than a little ridiculous wearing the red and green striped hat with pale, pointy felt ears. "Speaking of setting you up, I find it interesting that you both got together yesterday morning without my knowledge. Is there something I should know about?"

"Your brother seems like a really nice guy. But we've been over this before."

"Yeah, yeah. I know. Mari's your life. No complications allowed."

"Exactly. And by the way, you're wearing that all wrong." She reached over and yanked the hat down a few inches over so her ears were covered. "There. Now you're not some strange four-eared elf."

Kendra mock-saluted. "Yes, elf-Sergeant. And ring up the hat. I'm buying it and taking it with me. Oh, and a set of these peppermint things. I'm putting up my Christmas tree this week. They will go perfect with our all-red-and-white theme."

Sadie moved behind the cash register and rang up the purchase. As she made change for a twenty, she couldn't help but ask the nagging question. "So, where is Nate staying for the month? I can't imagine he'll want to live out of that hotel."

"No, he wanted a place with a kitchen and whatnot, and better WIFI. I told him it'd be impossible to find a place already furnished that had the whole month available, but he already found a few options online. The man is crazy good at that kind of stuff."

"I wish him luck. He's supposed to start helping with the play on Wednesday night."

Kendra picked up her sack containing her ornaments. "Well, I need to be off. I'm just so excited about having Nate here for Christmas I'm about to burst. He was never huge on celebrating Christmas, so this is the first time I'll have been with family over the holidays in years. I've always hung out with friends, but there's just something special about family, ya know?"

She did know. Even though Christmas tended to mix in with the rest of the year growing up, some of her most special memories were sitting around the tree with Mom and Dad, and later, with Mari. She wouldn't trade those for the world. The thought of spending Christmas without family was downright depressing. "Well, not this year. Nate will be here and it will be an amazing Christmas. And you'll come to the Christmas Eve service, right? If Nate's helping me…" She let the thought dangle, hoping Kendra would pick up where she left off.

Kendra tugged on an ear of her hat. "I—I don't know. I'll think about it, okay?"

Sadie couldn't stop the smile that spread on her lips. That was the best response she'd ever gotten. In the past, it'd always been a laugh followed by an, "*Um, yeah, NO.*"

"Well, I know Nate would love for you to be there, and of course, I would too."

A (kinda) Country Christmas

Her friend smiled, the sentiment not quite reaching her eyes, and waved as she walked out the door, the bell ringing behind her.

Sadie leaned against the counter and closed her eyes, her heart heavy. *Lord, this is turning out to be a really odd Christmas season. I have no clue what you have in mind here and where all this is headed. All I know is that Kendra is the sweetest woman I know, and there is so much hurt in her eyes. I'm not naive enough to think that going to a church building will cure all of her pain, but it'd be a start, right? And this whole thing with Nate— yeah. I don't even know how to pray for that, God. He's handsome and all, I'll give you that. But—*

The bell rang as the door ushered in a group of customers, their laughter filling the room.

For the best, probably, as her prayer was headed in a direction she had not meant to take it.

Best leave praying for Nate for another day.

10

N ate wiped his sweaty palms on his jeans as he stared at the little, white clapboard church, probably already bursting at the seams with the out-of-control tikes.

You're an idiot, Nate. They're just kids.

With at least one of them who liked to bite.

Man up.

Nate clenched his jaw. That's right. He was a man. Lots of men were fathers and dealt with this all the time. No reason he couldn't do the same. He would go in there, instill a little order, and teach them—

"Nate?" The front door to the church opened, and Sadie stood, tapping her foot, looking one part adorable with her hair in a high ponytail, another part sexy in her curve-hugging jeans, and a third part crazy with the most horrendous Christmas sweater he'd ever seen. "What are you doing standing out here in the cold? We're waiting for you."

"I was just on my way in." After sweating like a pig in twenty-degree weather for five minutes.

She lifted her eyebrows as he walked past her into the

A (kinda) Country Christmas

foyer. "Come on. We're meeting in the sanctuary today. The kids are really excited to meet you."

Too bad he couldn't say the same.

She gripped his arm and pulled him to face her. "Okay, spill it."

"What?"

"You look like you're about to face an executioner. What do you have against kids? I can't tell if you're the Grinch who hates kids or if you're just plain terrified of them."

Beads of perspiration formed on the back of his neck again. Why hadn't he worn a t-shirt instead of this long-sleeve button up? "I don't hate kids."

"Then what is it? The truth."

"It's a long story." It had probably started at the age of, oh, one day old.

"Give me the short, ten second version then."

"I've never been around a lot of kids." That was putting it mildly. "But I've been around a lot of men who come to work and complain about them. It doesn't leave the best impression on a guy." He wouldn't mention that he'd never been allowed to be a child himself. That his father had groomed him for business almost since the moment he exited his mother's womb. Playing with toys was rare and only done the few times a year they visited his Grandma Perry's house. His mom's mother had an attic room full of toys that she let him have free reign of while he was there. It was a treat more tasty than any ice cream ever could have been.

So yeah. The kids he had met, he couldn't relate to. Imagination? He hadn't even learned the meaning of the word until he was a teenager, and even then it was more making up stuff to get out of trouble. He'd had a pretty good knack for that.

Sadie's forehead dipped into a v-shape as her eyes drilled into his. She must have been okay with what she saw, because a moment later, the creases softened and a grin tugged on her lips. "Well, you're in for a treat then. We have a great group of kids and while they aren't always perfect, you won't be able to help but fall in love with them. Just keep an open mind and don't hyperventilate, okay?"

"Not promising anything."

Following her into the sanctuary, Nate stopped at the back pew and took in the transformation since Sunday. Children's voices vibrated off the walls, turning what was normally an orderly place of worship into a children's version of a loud, noisy pool hall.

Minus the smoke, alcohol and pool tables, of course.

Sadie grabbed his hand, gave him a wink of encouragement, and tugged him down the aisle. "Listen up, boys and girls. We have a special guest here today."

Bolstered by her hand grasping his, even if she did let go the moment they stepped onto the small stage, Nate crossed his arms and surveyed the little munchkins.

They didn't look nearly as dangerous as he'd pictured in his head.

In fact, most of them were smiling up at him with a look in their eyes he couldn't quite place.

Admiration? No, that couldn't be it.

Sadie clasped her hands together and addressed the group like an old pro. "This is Mr. Nate. He's here today because he's traveled all over the world for his job, so he knows quite a bit about how people in other countries celebrate Christmas. Isn't that cool?"

All the kids began talking at once, and one little boy who looked to maybe be six or seven popped up and shouted above the noise, "Hey, you ever been to Africa?"

A few others stood and shouted various countries.

Sadie flashed him an apologetic smile and clapped her hands in an odd rhythm. Like a magic spell had been cast in a church that definitely didn't believe in such a thing, the kids hushed. "Thank you for listening. Now, I'll let Mr. Nate say a few words and maybe give us a few examples of where he's been, then we'll get started."

Suddenly his mouth felt like it was stuffed full of cotton. If he wouldn't look like an idiot, he'd stalk off the stage and out the back door immediately.

They're just kids, Nate. You talk to large groups of adults all the time. This is easy in comparison.

But—for some reason, it wasn't.

He squinted and tried to picture the group of kids all in black business suits. Yeah, that actually helped a little. Clearing his throat, he stuffed his hands in the pockets of his khaki slacks and smiled. "Good evening. As Sadie mentioned, my name is Nate, and I travel more than my fair share. Show of hands, how many of you have ever been outside of the United States?"

Not one hand moved except one of the adult helpers. The woman laughed as everyone looked at her, and she shrugged. "Cancun on my honeymoon and Niagara Falls for our tenth anniversary."

Nate smiled and nodded. "Well, what if I told you I've been to more than twenty-five different countries?"

Little mouths flopped open all over the room.

"My job takes me lots of places, so to answer your question—I'm sorry, little man, what was your name?"

The boy who'd asked the original question piped up, his eyes glowing with excitement. "Peter, sir. Although Momma always says she regrets naming me after that apple guy because—well. Not sure why because but something 'bout how I'm always doing crazy stuff."

Nate looked at Sadie for an explanation. Apple guy?

She winked at him then addressed the boy. "The *apostle* Peter is a great namesake to have."

Ah. That made a little more sense. "Well, Peter, to answer your question, Africa is actually a continent and not a country, but I have been there, specifically to both Egypt and South Africa. I'm really excited to help you all out and can't wait to get started on your play." Laying it on a little thick, but surprisingly, it was more true than he would have imagined just a few short minutes ago.

The kids didn't seem to hate him. When he'd been younger, he'd been the quiet and boring kid who was fun to pick on. Now it seemed he was the cool world traveler they were in awe of.

He could handle that.

Sadie took back over and directed each kiddo into different groups. One section was kids with singing parts, another section had speaking parts, and the rest, the majority, were in the "angelic choir."

After the kids were in their areas, Sadie turned to him. "You're doing great."

He shrugged. It was no big deal, all he'd done was say a few words, but then why did he want to throw a fist in the air like he'd just gotten a bonus for saving a Fortune 500 company? "Thanks. Where do you want me?"

"How about with the older kids? They're practicing their speaking parts and could use a little help."

"But I thought you needed help with the actual material, you know, around the world stuff."

Her mouth tipped into a smile, a glint of tease in her eye. "We'll need your input, but that's more in set and costume design. Right now, kids need to memorize lines. Now, I need to scoot over to help our little angels with their songs. We have less than an hour before parents come to pick up their kiddos."

And with that, she disappeared into the sea of children.

Nate looked from her to the group of preteens staring at him, then back to Sadie again. Something didn't add up—

"Hey, Mr. Nate. You coming or should we go ahead and start?"

Stuffing his hands in his pockets again, he walked over. If you can't beat 'em, might as well join them.

11

"Hey, Mom, you have plans for tonight?"

Sadie looked up from the laptop where she'd been hoping to find a mistake in the most awful profit numbers she'd ever seen since Mom and Dad started letting her do the bookkeeping twelve years ago.

Nate's ten grand was certainly good timing, because the way things were looking, she wasn't even sure she'd be able to take a salary this month.

And December was supposed to be one of their best months.

At least the truck had gotten fixed without costing nearly what she'd feared. She'd expected to have to spend a chunk of the money on a new vehicle, but the mechanic said it was a belt or something. She knew zip about cars, so he might as well have been talking in Latin as he rambled off everything he'd done. All she'd understood was the final cost, and a few hundred bucks was music to her ears.

And she could still drive her dad's truck. Yes, it almost qualified as an ancient relic. And it might fall apart around her ears at any point. But every time she slid onto that old, vinyl bench seat, it reminded her of him. Of squeezing between him and Mom on the way to church on Sundays. It even still had that baked in smell of the Old Spice he'd always used.

"Um, hello? Earth to Mother?"

Sadie blinked and shook the random memories from her head. "Sorry, I'm—distracted. What did you need, sweetie?"

Mari stood over her, hands on her hips, her blond hair going to and fro as she shook her head. "I need to know your plans for the evening. It's Tuesday, so the shop will be pretty slow, right?"

Sitting back, Sadie tried not to laugh at this odd role reversal. What had gotten into her daughter? "Carla's closing tonight, but I was going to stay and catch up on some of the books." She *had* to have made a mistake somewhere. Things should not be this tight with Christmas a little over a week away.

Granted, she'd been more distracted than usual lately—it had nothing to do with Kendra's brother though.

Nothing at all.

So what if they'd been carpooling to church every Wednesday night for play practice and started a habit of having dinner together—with Kendra and Mari too—after church the last two Sundays. Kendra still hadn't come to church though, but had finally promised to come to the Christmas Eve service.

"Well, Kendra called and asked if we could all meet at Nate's place tonight around seven."

Sadie's heart did a little rebellious skip. Silly heart. It wasn't like it was his permanent house or something. It was just a cabin he was renting. Nothing more. Going to his place—with his sister and her daughter—was nothing to get all pitter-patter about. "Did she say what we'll be doing there?"

"Evidently he hasn't decorated for Christmas yet and

has no plans to. Says he can just come here or walk down the Parkway to get his fill of the Christmas spirit. Kendra said that was not acceptable. She thought we could all meet there and help him put up a tree and decorate, and have some hot chocolate and all that jazz."

Helping Nate deck his halls for Christmas? Oh yes. She was in. But— "How does Nate feel about all this?"

Mari's eyes lit up with a hint of mischief. "That's the best part. He doesn't know."

Sadie was afraid of that. What man would willingly let three women invade his home and decorate? Not many. And especially not Nate, Mr. Organized and Tidy. She'd decided the only reason he'd shaved his head bald was because he couldn't stand the idea of unorganized hair. "I don't know if that's such a great idea."

"But Kendra already has it planned. And I—uh—may have told her we could bring some of the decorations off the clearance shelf and donate them to the cause. I didn't think you'd mind…"

Sadie sighed. No, she didn't mind. It was a great idea, actually, except for the fact it was more inventory down the drain. But after his amazing gift, there was no way she could argue about helping him decorate for Christmas, and she knew just the ornaments to use. "That's fine. I'm still not sure about showing up at his house unannounced, though."

"Don't be such a party-pooper, Mom. He'll think it's funny and totally won't mind."

"You seem to be really all about this." Her daughter was usually trying to find ways to *not* spend time with her, not the opposite.

"Kendra and Nate are cool. I just think it will be fun."

It did sound fun. Maybe— "Fine. We can go."

Mari clapped her hands together. "Thanks, Mom. This is going to be epic. I can't wait to see Nate's face when we show up."

As her daughter all but danced from the room, Sadie

sat back and frowned. What had gotten into her daughter? Three weeks ago, she'd been a belligerent teenager who wanted nothing to do with her mother. And suddenly she was setting up outings for them together?

Something smelled a little rotten, but complaining about her daughter's behavior getting *better* seemed like crazy talk.

Maybe it was a Christmas miracle.

If so, this might be the best Christmas ever.

Nate took a right onto the back country road that led to his temporary Christmas cabin.

He was used to the city and noise and lights, but the past few weeks had shown him there was something to be said about the calm and serenity that could be found in the mountains.

Being able to come home to a quiet cabin with only the sounds of nature to greet him was relaxing.

Much needed after the crazy day he'd had.

His boss had called right after breakfast. They had a new client and needed someone to fly to Tokyo sooner rather than later to meet with them. It would be a quick trip, with the job not actually starting until the New Year. A six month assignment if their firm was hired.

Anxiety churned in Nate's stomach. Where were his Tums when he needed them?

A month ago, he would have agreed to the job without a moment's hesitation. But now—he probably would still go, but his confidence was dwindling.

A long drive in the mountains had cleared his head a little. Thankfully it hadn't snowed in over a week so the roads were mostly clear. The snow packed mountain peaks made for breathtaking views though.

But the clear air still hadn't calmed the restlessness that

A (kinda) Country Christmas

plagued him.

He glanced down at the clock on the dash.

Almost eight. No wonder his stomach was growling. He'd been too caught up in his thoughts to even think about dinner.

Maneuvering the SUV around the last curve, the cabin came into sight.

What—?

He tapped on his brakes, blinking his eyes. Had he turned on the wrong road? They *were* confusing.

What he *thought* was his cabin was—not.

Twinkling icicle lights hung from the front porch, and lights shined brightly from the windows.

Two vehicles were parked out front.

Then it registered. His sister's Jeep Cherokee beside a very familiar, very old truck.

He smelled Christmas rats.

Parking in the grass, the only spot left, he jammed the gearshift into park.

He'd specifically told his sister he was *not* going to decorate for Christmas. He wasn't even sure he'd be here now depending on how long it took in Japan.

He'd never decorated for Christmas. What was the point? Even after he got right with Jesus, he didn't see the purpose to the whole thing. Why did someone need lights to celebrate the birth of the Savior? Didn't that just distract from instead of add to the holiday?

Plus, it was just all—messy.

He was not a fan of messy. He didn't mind seeing it on the stores and whatnot. But his home where he relaxed was a different story.

Hopping out, he slammed the door with all the pent-up frustration from his day, stalked up the steps to the cabin, and flung open the door.

"Alright, what are you all—" The activity in the room halted, and the three women stared at him as if they'd been caught stealing Santa's toy bag.

All the anger and frustration fizzled.

Instead of messy and chaotic—the room was welcoming.

A Christmas tree stood in the corner, half decorated with none other than the same type of ornaments he'd ruined at Bethlehem's Boutique weeks ago. Green garland wrapped around the staircase and lined the fireplace mantle, and an off-white small nativity scene sat in the middle of the coffee table. The scent of cookies baking mixed with cinnamon and pine filled the air.

It was simple yet festive. If he were going to decorate for Christmas, this was the exact style he'd pick. A little country with a sprinkle of modern touches.

Kendra set down the ornament she was holding and wrung her hands together. "Well? What do you think?"

"I think—" What did he think? He'd come in here ready to give them what for, but now—it was all just—wow. "It's amazing. I don't know what else to say."

Sadie fidgeted with an ornament she held. "So you aren't mad?"

Not anymore. "Of course not."

Mari shook her head, her blond ponytail swinging behind her. "See Mom? I told you so. Only the Grinch would be mad over a Christmas surprise, and Nate here is definitely not that, right?"

Her eyes went to his, plunging him with guilt. He'd been mad when he walked in here. Maybe he did qualify for Grinch status. "Right." He shrugged off his coat and tossed it over the back of the recliner. "Now, how can I help?"

Kendra handed him an ornament. "Why don't you and Sadie finish the tree? Mari and I are going to go work on the cookies."

His stomach almost sang hosanna. "Cookies?"

Mari laughed and followed Kendra toward the kitchen. "Duh. We can't have a Christmas decorating party without Christmas cookies."

A (kinda) Country Christmas

Sadie shook her head and smiled while grabbing another ornament. "Yeah. Duh, Nate."

"Well, pardon me." Catching the Christmas bug, Nate picked up a clear glass ornament ball and shoved the decision he had to make into his mental figure-out-later stash. It'd still be there tomorrow. "Now, where does this go?"

"First, there is this lovely thing called a hook that you need."

He flicked her arm lightly. "I'm not completely Christmas-stupid."

She flashed him a saucy grin. "Sorry, but when your sister says you've never decorated for Christmas before, one has to assume you need detailed instructions."

He grabbed one of the curly doodads and attached it to the bulb. "Just because I never decorated doesn't mean I didn't see others do it. I'll have you know my parents hired the most illustrious interior designers money could buy to decorate the Meyers' place."

"Ah. That explains a lot."

He tried not to frown at what felt like a jab as he hung the glass ball in an empty space toward the top of the tree. He was used to the snotty-rich-kid jokes when he was a kid, but no one really understood just how bad they'd stung. "What do you mean by that?"

She picked up a faux white twig with little red berries at the end and inserted it expertly between tree limbs. "I just meant the whole never-decorated-for-Christmas thing. I wasn't sure if your parents were anti-Christmas or what."

His muscles relaxed. "No, but it definitely never revolved around Jesus, that's for sure."

They both reached for another ornament at the same time, and their hands brushed as they went for the same one. Sadie dipped her head, her almost golden hair covering what he was pretty sure was a beautiful, pink blush on her cheeks. "Sorry. I'll get a different one."

"Nope. It's all yours." He grabbed the one beside it as

he tried to ignore the tingling in his fingers. He'd held the hand of more women than he could count. Not a fact he was proud of anymore—but never had their close proximity had the effect on him that Sadie did.

He could feel his pulse pounding in his throat.

His palms were sweaty.

His hand fumbled with the ornament as he tried to keep still threading the hook.

No, this was definitely not typical Nate.

"You've gone quiet all of the sudden." Sadie had stopped and was staring at him, an amused smile on her face.

"Sorry. I'm—" Enchanted by your very presence and can't seem to stop acting like a fifteen year old boy with his first big crush? "I have a lot on my mind."

"Oh, what about?"

Desperate for an out, he grabbed the first thing off his for-later stash and threw it out there. "Work. I got a call today."

"And you usually don't get phone calls?"

"Not this kind. They want me to fly to Tokyo on Friday to visit a client."

A crash sounded behind them, and Nate turned to see Kendra, wide-eyed and pale. A plate of cookies lay scattered and broken on the floor.

12

"Y ou're leaving?" Kendra's bottom lip quivered as unshed tears filled her eyes.

Nate tossed the ornament he was holding onto the couch and crossed the room in three long strides, taking his baby sister in his arms. "I'm sorry, Kendy. I—"

She pushed him back. "No. I'm sorry won't cut it this time, Nate. You do this every year. I don't know why I thought this would be different."

Regret blasted through him like a rocket, destroying his heart in the process. They'd always done this over the phone. She'd beg him to spend Christmas with her, and he'd apologize and send her a big ol' gift to make up for it. It was easier that way at first. It's what Mom and Dad had always done. They'd rarely all been together for Christmas, and when they were, their parents were busy fighting or taking naps.

And more recently, his job had been an excuse to cover up the fact that he'd become just like his parents whom he'd despised.

Until this year.

Spending this month with Kendra, Sadie and Mari had

been like nothing he'd ever experienced. Helping out with the children at the church play—he'd felt included. Appreciated for something other than his business skills and robust bank account balance.

He wiped one of Kendra's tears with his thumb and shook his head. "It's just for the weekend. I fly out on Thursday and will be back home on Monday. I'll be back in plenty of time for the Christmas Eve play on Tuesday night." He'd be suffering from some major jet lag, but he'd survive. He always did.

She wiped her eyes with her shirt sleeve. "Promise?"

"Yes. I promise. Now. You ruined some good cookies there. I hope there are more."

Sadie had already cleaned up the mess on the floor, and Mari was carrying another plate from the kitchen. "Right here, hot and ready."

Kendra stepped back and tucked the stray strands of dark hair behind her ears. "Sorry guys. Geez, you'd think I was twelve instead of going on thirty, huh."

Sadie pulled her into a hug. "You're just fine. Plus, I was about ready to punch him at the thought of him skipping out on the play anyway, so you saved him from a black eye. He should be thanking you." She glanced at him and winked.

Kendra laughed. "Crap. If that's the case, I should have let you start swinging. That would've been hysterical."

"Ha ha." Nate grabbed a Santa shaped cookie from the plate Mari held and bit off his head. The flaky cookie mixed with red and white powered sugar icing melted in his mouth. "Mmmm. Delicious."

Kendra took a cookie and plopped down on the sofa. "We have hot cocoa or coffee ready too, if you want to help yourselves."

Nate followed Sadie into the kitchen. Funny how they kept being left or sent into rooms by themselves. Hm.

Sadie poured herself a mug of hot chocolate. "You want some, or do you prefer coffee?"

A (kinda) Country Christmas

"I'll take the hot chocolate for now, thanks."

She fixed him a mug and handed it to him. "So, Japan, huh? On such short notice?"

"Usually we can just do a conference over the Internet but this is a really important, potential client." From the way Sam, his boss, talked, it could be the defining highlight in Nate's career if he landed the account and was able to do the turnaround—with a six-figure bonus check attached if he succeeded.

And he *would* succeed.

If he took the job.

Was he really thinking of turning it down?

Anxiety made the hot chocolate he sipped taste more like sewer water. He shoved the project back where he'd originally had it. Later pile. "Enough about work. What do you say we go finish trimming the tree and steal a few of those cookies?"

"Sounds good to me. We should see if there are any Christmas movies on. Maybe watch one while we finish."

No Christmas movies were playing, but Kendra started jumping up and down like a teenager when she saw The Sound of Music was starting in ten minutes on one of the satellite channels.

As the women gathered around the tree, laughing and smiling as they put the last few decorations on, Nate hung back, leaning against a beam that separated the living and dining area.

This.

This was what Christmas was supposed to feel like. This deep down peace in his heart, a smile he couldn't turn off if he tried, the feeling of hope and joy brimming in his heart.

This is what he'd been missing all these years.

But—what was he supposed to do now? Quit his job and live a little country life in a touristy town in the middle of the Smoky Mountains? Settle down and get married and have a few kids?

Would that make him happy?

It was all well and good right now, a good old-fashioned country Christmas. He glanced around at the decorations, the modern and simplistic touches that were one-hundred percent Sadie.

Okay, so it was a *kinda* country Christmas. With a little bit of Sadie-sass mixed in.

But what about the day after Christmas?

What did he do then?

Lord, I could use some guidance here.

Because right now, my brain, my boss, and Japan are all calling my name, but a woman named Sadie, as crazy as it sounds, is calling my heart.

13

After the last of the kids were picked up by parents, Sadie plopped down in the pew beside Nate and rested her head back, eyes closed. "Phew. I'm beat. I can't believe this is our last practice before the play next week. I just hope no one forgets their lines between now and then."

"It'll be fine. You've done a great job with them." So great that he'd questioned more than once in the last three weeks why he'd even been invited to help. He wasn't complaining but—he did wonder. Those sets she'd mentioned him helping with? Yeah. They'd already been built. And a team of women from the church had handled all the costumes.

Her lips tipped into a shy smile. "Thanks."

Nate took the moment to study her profile, something he rarely got a chance to do for risk of being caught.

Beautiful. Her long eyelashes brushed against her skin, her nose turned upward to just the smallest bit of a point, and her lips—

He averted his eyes as not-so-church-worthy thoughts plagued him.

He hadn't ached to kiss a woman this badly in a long time.

Sadie had been perfect tonight, as always. She'd laughed and had fun but was obviously in charge, and the kids all adored her. She was a woman with so many layers and talents, he'd enjoy getting to peel back each one of them and find out what treasures lay beneath.

But—he reeled in his thoughts. They weren't his treasures to find. After the almost perfect evening last night, he'd spent this morning listing all the reasons pursuing Sadie was a horrible idea.

She wasn't the kind of woman who dated a guy like him.

She was good and he was—not.

She was country and he was—not.

She belonged here and he—didn't. As much as he wanted to, he knew that he'd go stir crazy after a while. He might last a few months, even a year. But deep down, he was just like his father. Business driven and not fit to lead a family.

All very good reasons he should get up and leave this pew immediately.

But not even a muscle in his body twitched at his command.

Lord, I know I probably look like a total idiot sitting here in your house with my eyes closed, but if I open them I might see him and throw myself at him or something really crazy like that, so I'm praying instead.

Sadie took a breath, trying to think horrible, awful thoughts instead of the blissful, kiss-filled ones that threatened.

Nate had been so *good* tonight. He'd come a long way from that first night when he looked like he might vomit all over his patent leather shoes. The kids adored him, and sweet Peter had taken to being his shadow, following Nate everywhere.

Then there was five-year-old Kallie. She'd tugged on his pants leg, and when he bent down, had asked if he was married. When he said no, she hugged his neck and declared that she would do the honors when she got to be old too.

Nate hadn't batted an eye before hugging her back and telling her she'd make a beautiful bride someday.

She'd skipped off to be fitted in her angel costume, happier than Sadie had ever seen her.

If there hadn't been children present, Sadie would have marched right over to him and kissed him on the spot.

Which was crazy. She shouldn't be feeling like this. Not for some guy who wasn't even close to her type.

What is your type then, Sadie?

Ugh. Maybe a cowboy kinda guy, or a ruggedly handsome mountain man with messy hair who wore plaid and drove a big black truck and prayed just as well as he played the fiddle.

It definitely wasn't a bald businessman who traveled the world and didn't even stay in a place long enough to have a real home and rarely connected with his family and who, until recently, didn't even like kids.

She could never be with a man like that.

It didn't matter that he was handsome and that his bald head was actually incredibly sexy. His light-green eyes that crinkled at the corners when he smiled didn't change a thing. Okay, so yes, he loved Jesus and that was definitely attractive. And his fear of the munchkins had actually been super adorable. And even though he was loaded money-wise, he obviously had no problem giving it away when God called him to. And just because she's always secretly dreamed of traveling around the world didn't change the fact that he wasn't the guy for her.

"Penny for your thoughts."

Warmth spread to her cheeks. Those particular thoughts would cost somewhere in the eight-figure range before they ever saw the light of day. "I'm thinking about my bed at home calling my name. It's been a long day." Maybe those weren't her *exact* thoughts, but they were true anyway, and she was thinking them now.

"You wanna know what I was thinking?"

She peeked one eye open. He had shifted in the pew, his eyes on her, a heat in his gaze she wasn't naive enough to miss. She really wasn't sure she should bite—but curiosity won out. "Sure."

"Why did you want me to help with the play?"

Not anywhere near the question she expected or feared. Sitting up, eyes wide open, she shook her head. "I don't understand. You've been coming all month. Pastor Silas told you—"

"Pastor Silas lied."

"Pastors don't lie, Nate."

"Well, he grossly over exaggerated then. I've watched you for three weeks now. You have this play and those kids running more efficiently than most companies I help, even after I'm finished whipping them into shape. You even wrote the play yourself, and you didn't need any help with the cultural details. So why am I here?"

"Well, I can't speak for Pastor Silas, but I think—" Boy, this was hard. "It was one part congregant retention and another part pastoral meddling."

She might as well have just suggested the pastor was Santa Claus himself by the look Nate shot her. "I'm sorry, what kind of retention?"

"I thought you of all people would get that part. He wanted you to stay. Feel welcome and included. It worked, didn't it? You've kept coming to church all month." And sat right beside her, sharing a hymnal, singing in his low but mostly-in-tune voice. She'd have to get used to sitting by herself again after he left. "And as far as the meddling part, I'm afraid his wife is a perpetual matchmaker—and he's been known to, ah, assist, her from time to time. In their defense, they have an excellent track record. I didn't have the heart to tell them how off base they were this time."

His gaze drilled into hers. "Yeah. That would be totally crazy."

Why couldn't she look away? Those crazy green eyes, they were the problem. They drew her in and made her want to find out all the secrets they held. She lowered her gaze but realized her mistake a moment later when his lips captured her attention. It'd been so long since she kissed a man. And really, Phin had just been a boy back then anyway.

Nate was no boy. He leaned forward, his spicy cologne luring her closer.

The first touch of his lips on hers was feather soft, as if he was taste-testing a decadent dessert.

His hand cupped her cheek, his fingers caressing her skin, sending ripples of pleasure clear down to her toes. His eyes probed hers, asking permission for more.

She should lean away. She should *run* away. They weren't right for each other. She should be focusing on Mari. On the boutique. On Christmas. On Jesus.

A man would only complicate her life, especially *this* man.

They didn't fit together.

Her body rebelled against her better judgment, leaning forward, anticipating, aching for more.

But just as their lips were about to meet again, Nate jerked back and stood up, grabbing his coat from pew.

Sadie sat, shocked, lips aching with want, heart bleeding. What had just—

"Ready for me to lock up, Sadie?" Pastor Silas's jolly voice boomed across the sanctuary.

Trembling, Sadie made a show of leaning down to grab her purse and coat she'd dropped on the floor. Hopefully the few seconds would give time for the flush to vacate her cheeks, but she knew it was in vain.

If Nate had seen the pastor, the pastor had seen them.

Lord have mercy, she'd just kissed a man in church. In front of the pastor.

Nate saved her by answering. "We were just leaving. Sadie, I'll be happy to walk you to your truck."

Finally standing, she refused to meet Nate's eyes, focusing on his ear instead. That was nice and safe. Sort of.

Good thoughts in church, Sadie. Come off it.

Turning, she waved to Pastor Silas, not able to find her voice to say goodbye, especially with the older man grinning ear to ear. It was like he routinely found a couple kissing in his church and blessed it.

Tugging on her coat, hat, and gloves, she braced herself against the cold as she made her way to her truck.

She was cranking the engine when Nate hopped into the passenger seat. "Phew, it's cold out there." He rubbed his arms with his gloveless hands.

"What are you doing?"

"Warming up. This cold air is brutal."

She tried not to smile. None of this was funny in the least.

But then why did she have this insane urge to laugh right now? "I'm serious."

He reached over and grabbed her hand off the steering wheel and squeezed it. "I don't—I needed to tell you I'm sorry."

That dreaded word few women wanted to hear after being kissed. "Sorry?"

He closed his eyes, a pained look stretching across his face. "I—I'm not the guy for you, Sadie. I'm sorry. I should never have let that happen in there. I got caught up in the moment."

Pain attacked her heart with the vengeance of a sword bent on inflicting death. He was right. Completely. She'd been telling herself all the same things.

But to hear it from his mouth—to know she could

never survive in his world. To hear the regret from the lips that only minutes ago she was kissing—

She shook her head. "No, I'm sorry. You're right. I'm—we're not compatible. You're this great, smart guy, world traveler, and I'm little ol' country girl Sadie. I—"

He brought her hand to his mouth and brushed a kiss against her knuckles. "It has absolutely nothing to do with you."

She pulled her hand back. "Sure it doesn't." *It's not you, it's me.* Classic line, even if it was full of bologna.

"If it wouldn't plague me with guilt for the rest of my life, I'd slide across this seat and show you just how much this is *not* about you."

White-knuckle-gripping the steering wheel to keep herself from sliding over to *him,* she stared at the little white church that had now gone dark, only a few electric candles lighting the windows. "Then why?"

A long silence filled the air, followed by Nate's sigh. "I'm not a good guy, Sadie."

That caught her attention. She glanced over to see his jaw flexed in a hard line. "What do you mean?"

"You know those guys your parents probably warned you about? The womanizers and men who never stay? The ones afraid of commitment and are pros at one-night stands? Well, you're looking at a professional one."

She shook her head. Nate? A professional player? That didn't jive with the guy she'd been around for the last three weeks, or the man Kendra claimed her brother to be. But—she'd been known to be fooled before. She didn't have the greatest track record with the judging the motives of men. "So—let me get this straight. You were kissing me in there with the hopes of getting me in your bed, then planned to dump me and leave?"

"Absolutely not." He grabbed her hand again and gripped it. "Five years ago I was in Paris working on a six-month assignment. About a month into it, I met a woman at a local club. Jade was full of life and energy and charisma. She lived life each day as it came and didn't have a care in the world other than having fun, which sounded great to me at the time. My job may sound glamorous, but fun—not so much. Jade was mysterious. I never knew her real name, only a first name I was fairly certain was fake. But after that first night, she'd show up at my flat at crazy times and—yeah. She was a fun distraction."

Sadie could fill in the blanks of what was going on. Part of her wanted to cover her ears and not listen anymore. She had sworn off "bad" boys years ago, and this new information about Nate sealed the deal on their incompatibility. But she couldn't help but feel the important part was yet to come. "So what happened?"

He turned to stare out the window. "She died."

Did he—no. Surely not. He wouldn't be confessing murder to her. Right? "How?"

"About three months into our—relationship if you could call it that, she stopped showing up. A week later, my client's company called a meeting. Aimee, the wife of the company's president, had committed suicide. It was so sad, but I didn't find out until I saw her picture in the newspaper. It was her."

This time, she squeezed his hand and scooted over in the seat, wanting to give comfort but not sure how. "I'm so sorry, Nate. That must've been difficult."

"I'd had no idea she was his wife. What really shook me was that she'd killed herself. I thought she was the happiest woman I'd ever met. Carefree, not a worry in the world. How could someone that happy on the outside be so miserable on the inside? Then I realized—I was just like her."

"Pardon me for saying—I haven't known you very long, but you don't seem like a happy-go-lucky, do whatever you want, kinda guy."

"I'm not. Not anymore anyway. I flew back to the states a month early and finished up the job remotely from New York. But I still couldn't reconcile who I was with

A (kinda) Country Christmas

who I wanted to be. A buddy of mine from work is a good Christian guy and was always inviting me to his church when I was in town. He took one look at me when I got back to the office and invited me. That time I accepted. I didn't change overnight, but I came to know Jesus and the peace that nothing else, not women or sex or even my career could give me."

Sadie wiped a tear from her eye. His story sounded much like her own, just in a different decade of life and minus a baby. "He changed you."

"He did. But—I'm not going to lie. I struggle. And you deserve better than that Sadie."

"In case you haven't noticed, I'm not the paragon of a sinless life myself."

"But you haven't—"

"I got knocked up when I was sixteen. Mari's daddy was a drug addict, and thinking back, I'm pretty sure he was a dealer too. He—he gave me a few free samples from time to time. When my parents found out about the pregnancy, they quit their jobs and moved us here."

"Where did you live before Gatlinburg?"

"Let's just say we lived in the ultimate Christmas town."

His arm, now flush with hers, vibrated with his chuckle. "And that is?"

"Santa Claus, Indiana."

He turned, releasing her hold on his arm, and shot her a look of disbelief. "You're kidding me."

"Nope. They'd lived there since before I was born. I was a very late in life baby. They'd been told they had no chance of having children, and so Mom thought for sure she was just going through menopause, but when she went to the doctor because of all her weight gain, she found out—surprise! She was forty-nine when I was born, and Daddy was fifty-five. They'd always loved Christmas and both worked in town as Santa and Mrs. Claus. Mom just told everyone she'd eaten a few too many of Santa's cookies to explain away her belly."

"That's—incredible."

"They loved me and doted on me, but honestly? I think they treated me more like a grandchild to spoil rather than a daughter to raise. I can look back and see it so clearly now. I never had a curfew, and the only discipline I ever got was my mom looking at me with her big, sad eyes and telling me she was disappointed at the choice I'd made. I had a lot of love and attention, but not much else. They were shocked when I told them about the baby. And they shocked *me* when they announced the following week that they'd quit their jobs and were moving us all down South to open their own Christmas store in Uncle Grant's old place he'd willed to them. It was their way of removing me from a bad situation. And believe me, Phin was bad."

"Phin?"

"Mari's dad."

Nate's arm slid behind her and tugged her closer. "I bet you were happy to move."

"Ha. You would lose that bet. I was livid and cussed my parents out at every chance I got. But then Mari was born. I don't know, there was just something about seeing her beautiful face and ten fingers and ten toes. I was smitten. I determined that day that I would protect my baby. That I would be a good Momma who raised her right, who taught her all about bad boys and how to avoid them. I would devote my life to her since I'd obviously ruined my own." But now her baby wanted to spread her wings. So where did that leave Sadie?

Alone.

That's where.

In a shop that sold Christmas stuff that she didn't even want to own anymore. In a town she would love to visit, but that didn't feel like home. In a house full of her parents' old furniture that wasn't even close to her style. In a truck that might blow up at any moment.

Nate's finger captured a tear that she hadn't even

realized she'd shed. "Your life isn't ruined, Sadie."

"No? How do you figure?"

"We're all saved through Jesus. We're all offered the same grace and redemption. I believe the Bible says somewhere in there that we're given new life when we accept Jesus."

True. Her life had definitely changed for the better when she'd finally accepted Jesus for the Savior he was. And wasn't that why she'd started to tell him her story anyway? "He's given you a new life too, you know."

He squeezed her shoulder. "I knew you were going to bring this back around to me somehow."

"I still don't know where this leaves—us." There. She'd said it. The word *us*. The one that signified there was something between them, more than a shared sister/friend, a ruined Christmas tree, and a children's play.

Nate leaned down and pressed his forehead to hers. "I don't know either. But I leave for Japan in the morning and get back on Monday. Tuesday is the play, and Wednesday is Christmas. Let's just enjoy the time we have for now, pray about it, and leave the rest up to God. What do you think?"

"Leaving the future in God's hands. Sounds very— wise. And Biblical."

His gaze dropped from her eyes and settled on her lips. "Do you think it would be unwise to finish what we started inside?"

Oh yes. Very unwise. Her body leaned closer to him, and her hand reached up to his chest to steady herself. The rapid thump of his heart beat a staccato against her palm. "Well, we're still in the church parking lot. So I dunno."

His lips were so close she could feel his warm breath tickling her skin. "We could always go park out in the street."

A giggle threatened to escape. "But then we might get hit by a car passing by. Plus, I don't recall ever reading 'Thou shalt not kiss in the church parking lot' in the

Bible." Very faulty logic....

"You're right. I think we're better off taking our chances here."

His mouth dipped until it covered her lips, and this time, there was no feather soft about it.

A (kinda) Country Christmas

14

Sadie finished tying the bow on the Christmas present she'd gotten for Nate and slid it under the Christmas tree. It wasn't anything big, just a pair of leather gloves to properly outfit him for winter.

Glancing out the window, she sighed at the sight of the moon high in the sky.

It was Saturday night, and the house was dark and quiet, Mari already in bed.

And sleep was nowhere close to happening for Sadie. Instead, she sat on the floor, knee deep in wrapping paper, hoping to get her mind off a certain man.

If she had any doubt Wednesday night about whether or not she and Nate had a possible future, she was completely sure now.

They'd never work.

Ever.

Like, ever ever.

She'd known him four whole weeks, and she was already beside herself with worry about him halfway across the globe. What if the plane went down? What if a war broke out, or a terrorist attack, and he couldn't get home?

What if he found some Japanese beauty who captured his heart?

Odd the whole trust thing. They weren't even officially dating, and she was already worried about him cheating on her, just from his description of his past.

But how stupid was that? It'd be like him worrying that she was out here smoking weed or something, which would be absolutely ridiculous.

None of that mattered though. They'd never work out if he traveled as much as he said he did. She'd worry herself into an early grave.

Grabbing another present, a scarf and earrings for Kendra, she put them in a small box, laid out the foil wrapping paper and measured her cuts.

She normally didn't wrap presents at eleven-thirty at night, but then again, she didn't normally worry about a businessman in Japan, either.

It would help if he'd do something crazy like call her or send her a message or something. She hadn't heard from him except for a quick text on Friday, letting her know he'd landed safely.

Of course, there was a time difference.

But it was, what, after noon their time?

He probably wasn't calling now because he assumed she was asleep.

He assumed wrong.

Why don't you call him?

She ripped a piece of tape from the dispenser and secured the paper on the backside of the box.

No. No way was she going to resort to showing him how desperate she was to talk to him.

He'd think she was some clingy woman who couldn't handle a few days alone.

That was definitely not her. She'd been walking on her own two feet since she was seventeen years old, with just a little bit of assistance from her parents.

Okay, maybe more than a little.

A (kinda) Country Christmas

But she was a grown woman.

Then why were her fingers itching to pick up her phone and dial?

Finishing the wrapping, she tied a shiny, wide purple ribbon around the present and made a bow on the top. She grabbed one of the homemade gift tags she made, wrote a little note, and attached it to the gift.

There.

The last of the presents wrapped. She'd already finished Mari's last night, and the small tree that sat in front of the front window looked complete.

Scooching back, she rested against the couch and pulled her cell phone from her pocket.

No missed calls. No missed texts.

Should she?

No. She'd already decided a future together would be insane. She could never do it. So why lead him on by calling?

Yet—she didn't want him to think she didn't care. Maybe she'd just call and leave a message. He was probably too busy to pick up anyway. She could just tell him she wanted to make sure he still planned on being home by Monday so he could come to the play Tuesday night. That the kids were counting on him.

Not her, of course. Just the kids.

Decision made, she clicked on his name in her contacts.

The phone rang three times and just as she thought voice mail would pick up, his voice filled her ear.

"Hey, beautiful. You're up late."

Her heart did a little pom-pom cheer of joy while her brain registered the mistake she'd made in calling. "I just thought I'd call to—uh—make sure you were still coming home on Monday." What had sounded like a great idea seconds earlier now sounded faker than fake when she voiced it.

"Sure you are. I'm sorry I hadn't called earlier. I've been in one meeting after another."

"Even on a Sunday?"

"Even on a Sunday. You're in luck though. We're in the middle of a break, and I'd just stepped outside for fresh air when you called."

Lucky her. "You never answered my question."

The low chuckle that came across the slightly fuzzy signal warmed her stomach better than any hot cocoa ever could. "Yes, I'll be home. My flight leaves tomorrow, and I'll get in there around ten on Monday. Then I plan to sleep pretty much the rest of the day."

She read between the lines. Don't expect to see him until Tuesday.

Which was fine with her.

Really.

"Okay. Well, good luck with the rest of your meetings."

"That's it?"

She hugged her knees to her chest. "What do you mean, that's it?"

"Come on, Sadie. You didn't just call me to check my arrival times. We both know it."

Fiddling with the hem of her snowflake patterned pajama pants, she searched for words, but nothing sounded right. She didn't want to get into this over the phone. "I just—wanted to say hi. Is that so bad?"

"Not at all. I've been wanting to say hi too, but afraid I'd scare you away if I called too much."

"You wouldn't scare me away but—I don't think this is working, Nate. I can't—"

"Shhh. Remember? Leave tomorrow to God. Let me get through this meeting and back home to you, and then we can talk."

Home? She wasn't even sure he realized he had used the word. A memory drifted to her of one of their first conversations, when he told her he didn't have a home.

Could that be changing?

Regardless, it didn't change her situation. "This is hard."

A (kinda) Country Christmas

"What is? Breaking up with me when we aren't technically even together? Or being apart from me and *not* technically being together?"

"I'm not even sure what you just said there, Mr. Smart business man."

"I like kissing you, Sadie."

Heat crawled down her spine as she touched her lips where, just a few days ago, his had been. "I like kissing you too." Truth, right there.

"I like talking with you."

"Me too."

"So let's just leave it at that for now. Will you spend Christmas Eve with me?"

"You know I'll be insanely busy at the store all day, then at the play in the evening."

"After the play, then."

"Not that I don't want to spend time with you, but Mari and I have a tradition of hot cocoa and singing Christmas carols at the top of our lungs then watching White Christmas. It is non-negotiable. And I'm sure Kendra wants to spend the evening with you."

"What if we did it together? Go back to your place after the play?"

The thought was too enticing. "That could work."

"Good. It's a date then."

"No, not a date. More like a—small Christmas Eve party."

"Let's not argue semantics. I need to get back inside, but I'll text you when I'm home, okay?"

No. It wasn't okay. But she agreed, said goodbye, and hung up.

Just lovely.

She was going to spend Christmas Eve with a guy who she really liked but had full intentions of breaking up with immediately after.

Although—could you break off a relationship that you never officially started?

Regardless, the ache in her heart that rivaled the miles between them in size told her that she had no other option.

Plus, she had Mari to consider. Her daughter needed her, whether she wanted to or not.

This little Christmas romance had been fun, but Mari was more important, and she had to put a stop to this before her heart got even more involved.

15

N ate sat in the second row pew beside his sister, something he hadn't ever thought possible.

His little sister, dogmatic agnostic, sitting with him in church, getting ready to watch little kids sing about the birth of the Savior.

If nothing else came from his relationship with Sadie, he would always remember this moment. Church wouldn't save Kendra. Only Jesus could do that. But it was a step in the right direction. He'd seen a softening in her lately, but then again, it was the first time in years he'd been around for more than forty-eight hours, so he wasn't an expert where his sister was concerned anyway.

Guilt knifed through him.

He should have visited more often. Stayed longer. She'd been a nomad for the last eight years after graduating college anyway, living in LA for a while, then New York and finally settling here.

Small town living seemed to agree with her, even though it was starkly at odds with how they both were raised.

The piano began playing, and Sadie entered from the

side door of the room, followed by a row of little angels.

They each found their taped off spots and stood tall, excitement glowing from their eyes. A few stood on tippy-toes and waved big when they found their parents.

Next came the rest of the actors and actresses, followed by the miniature Joseph and Mary, who carried a baby doll to represent Jesus.

The play went off with a lot of glitches.

Cute, adorable glitches that left not one face in the audience without a smile.

Peter sang at the top of his lungs during his solo, at one point forgetting the words and just making up his own.

One angel stole another's halo.

The halo-less angel sat down on the stage and wailed for Mommy, who quickly came and scooped her up and took her back to sit with her.

Half of the kids with speaking parts stood terror stricken in front of an audience and spoke with monotone voices, not the great acting they'd shown in rehearsal.

One kid shouted his lines instead of speaking them.

But there wasn't a bone in his body that could be prouder of those kids. He'd only been there the last four practices, but he was invested in them. His heart already loved every single child.

They were no longer scary. He understood now why Jesus had welcomed the children.

The play came to a close with a moving scene of a shepherd kneeling before the baby doll Jesus and kissing him on the cheek while the angels sang Hark the Herald Angels Sing.

Sadie had wanted to end the play with that, because regardless of how your culture celebrated Christmas, it should all point back to the birth of the King of Kings, Love's gift to the world.

The congregation clapped as the kids took bows and rushed to sit with their parents.

The lights dimmed, and Sadie slipped into the pew

beside him as the music director began to lead them in "O Holy Night."

He pressed a hand to her back and leaned in to whisper. "You did a great job."

She mouthed *Thank you* then sang along.

This.

Right here.

This moment was perfect. His sister, the last remaining family member he knew, on one side. And on the other side, the woman who, crazy as it sounded, had captured his heart.

He'd had a lot of time to think and pray on the plane.

And considering how dismal his Tokyo meeting had gone, he had never been surer of a direction God was leading him.

His divine finger was pointed directly at this sweet, amazing, passionate, courageous woman standing next to him.

The woman he had gone and fallen in love with.

16

The house was quiet as Sadie snuggled under Nate's arm on the couch, enjoying the warmth he offered even as her mind shouted all the million reasons she should have insisted Mari stay downstairs until he left. Kendra had claimed exhaustion and left a few minutes ago.

It was Christmas Eve, though. For the next hour anyway.

She could enjoy this feeling one last time, right?

They'd had an amazing evening. The play had been nothing short of hysterical. Then Kendra and Nate had added the perfect touch to the traditional Christmas Eve gathering, Nate belting out carols like a pro and even enjoying White Christmas, claiming he'd never seen it before.

She hadn't known there was a person left in the world who hadn't seen the iconic movie.

Bing Crosby and Rosemary Clooney reminded her of Mom and Dad, especially at the end all decked out in their gorgeous red suit and dress. Classy and full of smiles.

That had been her parents. What she wouldn't give to see her dad decked out in his Santa suit just one more time. Maybe that would be odd for most people, but it was normal for her.

Man she missed them.

Nate stroked her arm with his thumb in circular motions, the fire crackling, adding just the right touch of ambiance. "If you could do anything, Sadie, what would it be?"

Stay in this moment forever. "What do you mean?"

"Let's say the boutique wasn't an issue and you could pick anything, what would you do?"

Give up the boutique?

Even the thought sent shivers of some emotion she wasn't sure how to describe. Fear, excitement, exhilaration, all wrapped into one. Could she really set aside her parents' dream?

"I think—I honestly don't know. My parents loved that store. They always dreamed—"

"But I'm not asking about their dreams. I'm asking about yours. What are the gifts God has given *you*? If money and Mari and your parents and the boutique weren't an issue, and it was just up to you, what would you do?"

She studied the fire, the flames licking at the logs, and searched her heart. Was she really so one-dimensional that she had no big dreams of her own? Had she really put all her eggs in other people's baskets?

Nate shifted so he caught her gaze, then lifted her chin with his finger. "Let's try this. What are a few of your favorite things?"

She smiled at his *Sound of Music* reference from last week. The man had been listening. "I think—children. I love kids. Maybe it was being a mom so early in life, but I've always been drawn to children and their innocence, you know? I loved working with the kids on the play these last few months."

He leaned down and pressed a kiss to the corner of her mouth, his eyes twinkling. "Are you saying you want to be a mother again?"

Her cheeks burned hot at the suggestion. Her? A mom again? "I'm—I've honestly never thought about it before. So no, that wasn't what I was saying. I can't imagine going through all those stages of motherhood again." But she *was* only thirty-four. Half the women her age were just starting out having children these days.

"It'd be different this time though."

She laughed. "Oh? You're an expert in child rearing now too?"

"You know me. Kid at heart. But you went through it alone last time, not to mention you were still a kid yourself."

She shook her head. This conversation was veering out of control. "Well, it's a moot point anyway. I'm not married and that would have to happen for me to even consider such a thing. No—maybe a teacher? I'd be good at that, I think."

"So, what's stopping you?"

Leaning away, she twisted to look at him. "Uh, how about everything? I own a Christmas boutique that will barely keep the lights on this month. I have a daughter going to college next year and no way to pay for it. I'd have to go to college myself when I barely got my GED eighteen years ago." She pushed away. The warm fuzzies of the evening had fled the room as reality slapped her in the face. "Listen, Nate. I know you mean well. But—you were right the other night, you just had all the wrong reasons. It has nothing to do with my past or your past. We're just—two different people. Living different lives that don't fit together. I'd never make it knowing you were off gallivanting around the world to who knows where for months at a time."

He didn't move an inch, but she could see the muscle in his jaw tighten.

"And then there's Mari. Even if we did figure out how to make this crazy relationship work, I refuse to leave her.

A (kinda) Country Christmas

She's going to UT Chattanooga next year. I want her to have a place to come home to. She's my whole world, and I can't uproot her and leave her with no familiar place to go."

"The world doesn't revolve around your daughter, Sadie. She has to make her own place in it."

"That's just it. *My* world does. I can't just send her off and say, I fell in love, sweetie, so see ya later. Good luck with life."

"No one is asking you to do that."

"Then what *are* you asking me to do?"

He reached up and fingered a strand of her hair. "To snip off the string you have her tied to and let her fly. To let yourself fly."

She stood up and propped her hands on her hips. Walking over to the wall that held Mari's baby pictures, she shook her head. "That's ridiculous."

"Is it? She's eighteen. She already graduated high school. She should be off enjoying college and starting a new chapter in her own life now, not sitting at home, worrying about her mom being lonely."

Sadie spun around. "How dare you."

"How dare I what? Tell you the truth?"

She pointed a trembling finger toward the front door. "Get out."

"Sadie—"

"I said get out. Now."

He stood and stuffed his hands in his pockets. "I'll leave after I say one last thing." His eyes drilled into her as if he were digging for gold. "I love you, Sadie Jenkins. I know it's crazy and probably too soon to tell you that, but it's the truth. I have no idea how we'd figure it out, but there is no future for you period when you've already closed off your heart and marked it 'Mari only.'"

A moment later, he was gone.

Sadie stood, staring at the closed door, listening to the car door slam, then tires crunch in the snow as he drove away.

A noise from upstairs grabbed her attention. "Mari?"

Silence.

Making her way back to the living room, she dropped to the couch and buried her face in her hands.

Was he right?

Maybe.

But—what did "cutting the string" look like? Mari was already set to finally go to college in the fall, but the boutique was supposed to help her save up money.

What would Mari do if she just up and closed the boutique come January? For that matter, what would *she* do?

There were so many questions and zero answers.

She sat there and stared at the fire until it died down to ashes, no loud booming voices giving her direction, and no soft whispers either.

Just silence.

She glanced at the clock.

Quarter after one. Christmas morning had come.

Curling up on the couch, she tucked the throw pillow under her head and pulled the blanket she kept handy over her.

In the fleeting moments before sleep arrived, she finally recognized the searing pain that wouldn't let go.

It was the cruel sensation of her heart breaking in two.

17

L ight attacked her eyes, shaking her from an odd dream that was just out of grasp.

Sadie stretched and moaned, wincing at the loud crack that came from her back.

She kicked off the blanket her legs were tangled up in and stood, stretching again.

Her eyes caught sight of the presents under the tree.

Ah. Yes. Christmas morning. None of the typical excitement she usually felt was present at the thought.

Her brain jolted as her eyes caught the light streaming in from the front window.

It was Christmas morning, and Mari hadn't woke her up at the crack of dawn, as she had every year for the past sixteen-ish years.

"Mari?"

No response.

Fully awake now, she pounded up the stairs. They'd been up late. She probably had just overslept, too.

Knocking on her door, she jumped when it opened under her hand. Peeking in, she frowned. "Mari?" The covers were rumpled, but the bed was empty.

She checked the bathroom.

Empty.

Her heartbeat thudding in her throat, she ran down the stairs. "Mari! Where are you?" Maybe she'd been in the kitchen or—

A little white piece of paper on the small table by the front door caught her eye.

Grabbing it, she collapsed on the floor as she scanned the note.

It's time for me to fly, Mom. Merry Christmas. Love, Maribelle.

No, no, no.

She buried her face in her hands. Mari must have heard her and Nate last night.

Nate. This was all his fault. Well good, then he could help Sadie find her. She stood up and reached to grab her keys from the hook by the door only—

They were gone.

One glance out the front door confirmed.

Her little bird had flown away in Sadie's only vehicle.

Of course.

At least she wasn't walking or taking the bus or something. Sadie could be thankful for that anyway.

Fishing her phone out of her purse, she clicked Nate's name and tried not to panic as the phone rang. He answered on the second ring. "Merry Christmas."

"She's gone."

He paused. "Who's gone?"

"Mari. She left a note. I think she heard us talking last night. She took my truck and is gone."

"Hold on. I'll be right there." A click and dead air followed.

She stuffed her phone in her pocket then realized, duh. She could always *call* her daughter. Clicking on the smiling face framed with beautiful blond curls, Sadie prayed Mari would answer.

But the call went straight to voice mail. "Mari, this is

mom. Please call me. I'm worried sick. Love you, sweetie. And—Merry Christmas."

Tossing the phone onto the couch, she paced the floor. Should she call the police? Alert the news station?

No. That was dumb. Mari was eighteen and had left a note. She legally wasn't running away or doing anything wrong, except, of course, stealing her mother's truck.

And there was no way she'd report her own daughter for theft.

Let her fly. Let yourself fly.

Nate's words from last night haunted her.

What if he was right? What if instead of protecting her daughter, she'd just been grasping tight and stifling her, not letting her stand on her own two feet?

What if—what if she was afraid she didn't know how to fly without her daughter?

She'd devoted every minute of every day to Maribelle for eighteen years, her attention only distracted by helping to run the boutique, but even that was to be able to pay bills to fund all Mari's activities and put food on the table.

After a few minutes of pacing, the front door opened.

Sadie whipped around, but instead of Mari, Nate stood there. Two quick steps and he was bundling her into his arms. "I'm so sorry, Sadie. This is all my fault."

She couldn't even respond except to burrow herself deeper in his embrace.

Oh it felt good not to be alone right now. To be held in his arms and have someone else to worry with her. For a moment, she let him hold her up and support her. Burying her face in his t-shirt clad chest, she inhaled his scent. Clean and soapy, minus the cologne he usually wore, but still masculine and still a hundred percent Nate. "It isn't your fault."

He pushed her back to look in her eyes but didn't let her go. "Yes, it is. I should have realized she might hear us and take what I said the wrong way."

"I think she realized you were right."

He slid a hand across her cheek and tucked her hair behind her ear. "How so?"

"I think I've just been so afraid of losing her and being on my own, that I was holding on too tightly. But she's her own woman now. And maybe it's time I be my own woman too."

"That sounds very wise."

She pushed out of his embrace and wrapped her arms across her chest, a shiver of cold spiraling through her core.

Nate glanced at the door. "Sorry. Forgot to close it." He walked to shut it, then stopped. "Sadie, did you call anyone else?"

"No, not yet. Why?"

He pointed out the door. She came up behind him to see the most glorious sight in the world.

Two vehicles came up the drive. A gray Honda sedan she'd never seen before, and behind it, Dad's old truck.

Not caring about her bare feet, she ran out to the snow-covered sidewalk to meet Mari jumping down from the cab of the truck. Sadie didn't waste even a second before crushing her in a hug. "Don't you ever do that to me again. You scared the daylights out of me."

Mari squeezed her back. "Sorry, Mom. I just needed to think a little, I guess."

Sadie let out the breath she felt like she'd been holding for the last twenty minutes. "I know, honey. I'm sorry. I should have let you fly a long time ago."

Nate called from the doorway. "Might wanna get back inside. Your feet are going to get frostbite."

Sadie grabbed Mari's hand and scurried across the snow to the front door. Her feet were numb at this point anyway.

Once they were inside, Mari paused. "Uh, Mom? There's something I need to tell you."

Sadie braced herself. Mari's expression scared her. She looked—worried. And a little guilty. *Oh, Jesus, please no—*

A (kinda) Country Christmas

"It's okay, Honey. You know I'll still love you no matter what."

Mari wrinkled her nose. "What? Oh my gosh Mom, I'm not like pregnant or anything. I was gone for a whole eight hours. Geez."

Relief flooded her. Not that she really thought that but—well. She was pretty sure she'd worn that same expression when telling her mom about Mari all those years ago. "Then what is it?"

A knock sounded on the door that Nate had discreetly closed.

Sadie looked at it, then at her daughter. She'd forgotten about the second car. "Are you—dating someone then?" *Lord, I'll be okay with this as long as he loves you and doesn't do drugs—please!*

"No, I'm not dating anyone. You trained me well to just be friends with boys until I was ready for something more."

Sadie let go of her daughter and walked to the door. "Then who is visiting on Christmas morning?" She flung open the door to see—

The world spun for a moment at the familiar face that had filled her nightmares for so long.

How could—

No. She blinked. Was she still dreaming? Another nightmare?

A strong arm pulled her back against a solid body and supported her. *Nate.*

She glanced back at her daughter who was biting her nails, a tell-tale sign of nerves and guilt, then back at the man who she hadn't seen in almost nineteen years.

"What are you doing here, Phin?"

18

"**M**erry Christmas, Sadie. It's been a long time."

Gripping the doorknob, she motioned for him to come in. Not that she wanted to. She'd love nothing more than to slam the door in his face and never see him again.

But if her world was going to crumble underneath her, she'd like to at least understand why. "You didn't answer my question. Why are you here?" She shut the door behind him and straightened her spine.

"Mari invited me."

Nate's hand on her waist and gentle squeeze was the only thing that kept her from yelling *liar* at the man. "That makes no sense. Mari doesn't even know you."

Her daughter stepped forward, an arm wrapped around her stomach. "Actually, I meant to tell you, Mom."

Sadie blinked and shook her head. "Tell me what? I don't understand." She'd always been honest with Mari. At first, she'd told her that her daddy was young and not ready to be a daddy. As she got older, she'd explained that her daddy had made some really bad choices which made him not be able to be a good daddy anymore. And in high school, they'd talked about drugs and how they ruined lives, her daddy's a prime example.

She'd given her a small old high school picture of Sadie and Phin, the only one she had. Mari kept it in one of the drawers of her jewelry box.

"I looked him up over the summer. Online. You'd already told me his name, and I knew he'd gone to high school with you, so it wasn't that hard. I found out he lives in Knoxville and got his email address."

Sadie blinked. Her daughter had done all this behind her back? "But—why? Weren't you happy here?"

Mari brushed away tears with the palm of her hand. "Of course I was, Momma. But—a girl wants to know her daddy too, you know? And so when I found him, I couldn't help it. Did you know that I have two sisters and a little brother? We've been emailing back and forth for the last six months, just getting to know each other. I—I wanted to tell you, but I was afraid you'd get mad."

And she would have. She was. Kinda. She looked from Phin to Mari, then back to Phin again. He looked— normal. Like a typical thirty-something guy, trim, a few early gray hairs speckling his black hair. His eyes were clear and serious, not distant and cloudy from drugs.

Phin looped his thumbs through his belt loops. "I'm sorry to barge in like this on Christmas morning, but when Mari showed up this morning, I told her you'd be worried sick about her."

"Have you—have you two met before this then?"

Mari shook her head. "No. Phin—I mean, Dad— thought I should tell you first. But I didn't know where else to go this morning. I sat outside his house for over two hours before I had the courage to knock on the door."

"Listen, I need to be going back. Sadie, I—I'm sorry. I've been wanting to tell you that for years, but never felt right intruding on your life after I left like I did. But I really am sorry for how I treated you. I was a messed up kid who was running as fast as I could away from God. I've already apologized to Mari for missing out on her growing up, and she's forgiven me. I just—I'm really sorry."

She blinked away tears and sniffed, desperately trying not to completely come unglued in front of everyone. "I—forgive you." And she did. Truth be told, she was a pretty lost kid herself back then.

He reached out a hand, and she met his grip and shook it.

"Merry Christmas everyone." And with that, Phin was gone.

Mari stood, her chin down.

Sadie left Nate's silent but strong presence to wrap her arms around her daughter. "You know that I love you, Maribelle Renee Jenkins, right?"

Mari sniffled against Sadie's shirt. "I know, Momma. I'm sorry."

Setting her away, she wiped her daughter's tears with her fingers. "Now stop that. No crying on Christmas unless they are happy tears. I think we should open presents, what do you think?" Talking could come later. But that would need to be a no-boys-allowed, PJ's and popcorn type of talk.

They spent the next hour taking their time, opening gifts, and finished off with Nate reading the Christmas story from Dad's old Bible. They headed to Nate's for lunch, where Kendra had already stationed herself, making the most delicious Christmas ham Sadie had ever tasted.

The afternoon passed in lazy fashion, watching old movies and Nate beating the socks off everyone in checkers.

When Mari declared she was tired at a mere six pm, Sadie stood from the couch to leave, but Kendra hopped up. "I'm going right by your place on my way home. I'll just drop her off so you don't have to rush."

Her little townhouse wasn't even close to on the way to Kendra's mountain home. "That's okay. I need to—"

A (kinda) Country Christmas

"Fly." Mari stood behind her and whispered the little word in her ear, then grabbed her purse and followed Kendra out the door.

"Looks like we've been ganged up on." Nate sat on the edge of the couch, folded the checkerboard and tossed the pieces into the box, then slid it on the shelf under the coffee table.

Busy work to keep his mind off the woman he had confessed to being in love with last night after she kicked him out of her house.

Not one of his brightest moments.

"I think you're right."

He sat back on the couch and patted the seat next to him.

She sent him a wry smile and sat, keeping a good five inches between them.

That would never do. He reached behind her and tugged her to him, settling her into the curve of his arm. "That's better."

She didn't answer except to curl her feet up behind her and snuggle into him.

Bliss. Pure and utter bliss.

He propped his feet up on the table, clad in the crazy elf-like Christmas socks Kendra had gotten him for Christmas.

"Cute socks."

He wiggled his toes. "I'm afraid Christmas socks are going to be an annual gift from her, now."

"Maybe she'll twist it up from time to time with a Christmas sweater or something."

"I think we'll stick with the socks, thank you. Enough about my footwear and crazy sister, though. How are *you* doing?"

She toyed with a button on his shirt as she sighed.

He pushed away the image that played with his mind at her innocent motion. He didn't have a right to that train of thought—yet. He gently grabbed her hand and threaded his fingers through hers. A little safer. Barely.

"I'm doing okay. Today was just a lot. But—I've been thinking."

He squeezed her hand. "Thinking is always good." Usually. Most of the time.

"You were right about me."

He'd spent half the night praying for Sadie and Mari and their future. If Jesus was here, Nate would give him a giant hug and back slap right now. "Oh?"

She squeezed his hand. "Now don't get all cocky on me. I still don't know how all—this would work out. But I do know that I need to let Mari fly and need to explore what that means for me."

He let go of her hand and brushed her cheek with his fingers, bringing her gaze to meet his. "Why don't you know how all this will work out?"

"You're going to be gone for what, six months after the first of the year? And not just across the state, but across the world. I don't know if I can be the woman that does the whole long distance thing. And—there is a lot still to figure out here. Even if I close Bethlehem's boutique, I still need an income. It's the only income Mari has right now too. I just—"

"Marry me."

Her words jammed to a stop and her body tensed at his side. "What did you just say?"

What *did* he just say? He was not a rush-into-things kinda guy. That's how mistakes got made, how businesses failed.

But this wasn't a business. It was the rest of his life. And deep in his heart, he knew it wasn't a mistake. He'd just planned to initiate it a little more eloquently. "I turned down the Japan job. In fact, I put in for a transfer to an open position stateside in our Nashville office. It isn't as close as Gatlinburg, but it's only a few hours north of Chattanooga, so you'd still be in driving distance to Mari. And I might still have to travel some, but nothing like I do now."

She disengaged from his arms and stood up, wringing her hands together. "That's—great. But—"

He stood up beside her. "But what, Sadie? What are you afraid of?"

"I'm afraid I'll say no and regret it the rest of my life."

"Then say yes."

"But what if I say yes and a year down the line, regret that too?"

He slid a hand behind her neck and brought his lips to her forehead, kissing over top of her bangs. "I can't promise you we won't fight, baby. I can't even promise you there won't be moments you'll want to kick me to the curb. But I will promise to always love you and cherish you. To be the husband I never thought I'd be able to be. To honor our marriage and honor you, and most of all, honor God. There is not a thing that would change that between now and next month or next year. I'd love nothing more than to spend the rest of my life getting to know every detail about the woman I love."

She reached up and ran her finger across his lips, sending shudders of pleasure down him. "Say it again."

He raised his eyebrows. "The whole thing?"

A smile touched her lips as she swayed forward, closing the small gap between them. "No. The part about you loving me."

Pressing his forehead to hers, he looked into her deep, blue eyes. "Sadie Jenkins, I'm madly in love with you. I love the way you giggle when you laugh, even without knowing it. I love the way your eyes sparkle when you're talking to a child, and how you love them well, regardless of how rascally they are. I loved the way you scowled at me when I broke your tree—"

She tossed her head back and laughed. "Hold on a second. You did not love that."

He cupped his hand to her cheek and pulled her back. "Wanna make a bet? You are cute when you scowl."

"Liar."

"See? Right there. Most adorable scowl in the world. And remember, I'm experienced in such things. Although, I have to admit your smile is just as beautiful and a little less terrifying."

That bought him a soft punch in the stomach.

"The bottom line is, I love you, Sadie." He reached into his pocket and brought out the gift he'd been wanting to give her all day, been praying about the wisdom in giving it to her. He'd thought after last night that God was telling him no.

But then today happened.

A true Christmas miracle.

Dropping to one knee, he held out the little black box wrapped in a simple red bow. "Would you, Sadie Claudia Jenkins, do me the great honor of becoming my wife?"

He held tight to her trembling hand as she wiped a tear from her eye with her other. "I—I love you too, Nate. Yes. Yes I'll marry you."

Not even caring that she hadn't seen the ring, he tossed the box onto the couch and stood, capturing her into his arms. Before he could make a move, she brought her lips to his and entwined her arms around his neck, her body flush with his.

Suddenly the empty house seemed very—tempting. It took all his strength to gentle the kiss and put a few inches between them. His voice sounded raspy, even to his own ears. "When?"

Her eyes danced with a heady passion that was getting harder to resist. "When what?" She swayed toward him and kissed him again.

Against every desire coursing through his body, he pecked her lips and rested his forehead against hers. "New

A (kinda) Country Christmas

Years Eve."

Sadie snapped her head up, Nate's words registering. "What?"

"You heard me. Marry me. On New Year's Eve."

He couldn't be serious. "Like, next week or next year, New Year's Eve?"

His eyes bored into her with a pleading look. "Please don't make me wait a year, Sadie. I'll be moving to Nashville for my job and setting up a home, a real home, and there is nothing that would thrill me more than to have you by my side. You said yourself, a long distance relationship would be difficult."

She had said that. And the thought was oh-so-tempting. But there were a lot of things to consider. "What about me? I know you have your job and—you know I love you, Nate, but I would make a horrible professional homemaker. I've worked all my life."

"Then we'll hire someone to come in and clean. You can go to college and work on that teaching degree you talked about. Or—" he wiggled his eyebrows playfully. "We can always discuss that other idea."

Kids. She had never contemplated the idea of having more children. But with Nate—he'd make one handsome daddy, that's for sure. "I'll have to think on that."

He tilted her chin up gently with his fingers and pressed his lips against hers with the most gentle of kisses. "So what do you say? Can you plan a wedding in a week?"

She had no clue how she'd pull it off. There were so many things to consider. They'd have to keep it small—but then again, small fit her just fine.

Fly, Sadie.

Was getting married immediately really flying though, or just tethering her string to another person?

She closed her eyes and pictured her and Nate, flying through the air, hand-in-hand.

Maybe it didn't have to be either-or. They could just fly together.

"Can I see my ring first?"

He laughed as he reached down and grabbed the little black box from the couch and loosened the ribbon. "Of course."

She gasped as he opened it to reveal the most beautiful diamond solitaire she'd ever seen, a perfect round shape, just as she would have picked. "It's breathtaking."

Taking her hand in his, he slid it on her left ring finger. "So what will it be, future Mrs. Meyers?"

"I think a New Year's Eve country wedding sounds fabulous."

"We could always rent out a barn and have a good ol' fashioned hoedown for the reception."

She laughed and shook her head. "Okay, maybe only *kinda* country. I was born in Indiana, remember. I wouldn't know how to two-step to save my life."

"So Indiana with all its corn is the hub of bustling city life now?"

"Shut up. You know what I mean."

He chuckled and drew her closer, then slid a finger down her cheek, ending with a tap on her chin. "Okay. Scratch the barn idea then. As long as you, me, Mari, Kendra and the Pastor are there, I'll be a happy man."

"Sounds like an excellent plan to me."

He leaned down to kiss her again, but she drew back when another thought popped into her head. "Hold on a minute. A little bit ago, you called me by my whole name. Who told you that?"

A guilty grin tipped his mouth upward. "A little bird."

She groaned. "Mari is in so much trouble."

"It actually answered a lot of questions I'd had."

"Oh really?"

"I'd wondered why, since your parents were the ones all

about Christmas, they hadn't named you a more Christmasy name like you did Mari."

Her embarrassment was complete. "Well, now you know. Sadie Claudia was the only girl name they could think of that came anywhere close to Santa Claus. And don't you dare tell Maribelle this, but her name was out of pure spite. I figured since she was going to be born in the south and be the granddaughter of Santa and Mrs. Claus, she should have a Christmas *and* southern belle name. Maribelle did the trick."

"I think it's cute."

"I think so too. Sadie Claudia, however, not so much."

"We'll just have to agree to disagree on that." And with that, he broke off any rebuttal she might have had with a kiss that sent shivers of pleasures clear to her toes.

A New Year's Eve wedding was sounding better and better by the minute.

Krista Phillips

Did you enjoy
A (kinda) Country Christmas?

Please consider sharing your thoughts with other readers by posting a review online. Amazon.com or Goodreads.com are great places to share your thoughts with other readers looking for great fiction!

Krista Phillips

A (kinda) Country Christmas

Acknowledgments

HUGE thanks to –

My hubby and kids – you deal with way too much macaroni and cheese for dinner and fishing clean clothes out of laundry baskets as I follow this writing journey— THANK YOU for loving me anyway!

Jessica E – YOU ROCK! Thanks for being such a GREAT reader and giving me feedback in a pinch!

All the Love's Gift authors – It was an honor to have my little book alongside your brilliant stories!

The Alley Cats – I couldn't walk this journey without you girls, sisters of my heart!

Sarah Forgrave – If this book stinks, I blame you (not really...but you get my drift!) I can't believe I'm publishing a book without you reading it first! *sniffle* But you're gonna whip all our booties in shape so I'll muddle through!

The Town of Gatlinburg – I know this is just a small little book, and I couldn't highlight the awesomeness of your little town as much as it deserves, but our family loves visiting and I enjoyed visiting in my fictional little land too! Any errors I made—we'll chalk it up to my imagination!

And to *Jesus*, God's gift to the world. We don't deserve you, but you came anyway. We mocked you, and you loved still. There was no "kinda" about it.

Krista Phillips

A (kinda) Country Christmas

Also by Krista Phillips

"With the message that it is never too late to turn back to
God, this faith-filled romance is absolutely impossible to put
down. Phillips's entertaining, heartwarming, and compelling
love story will satisfy admirers of Francine Rivers and Susan
Anne Mason.— Library Journal Starred Review

Want to find out more about Krista and her books?

Visit and connect with her online at:

www.kristaphillips.com
www.facebook.com/AuthorKristaPhillips
Instagram - @kristajeanphillips

7